BANDOLERO

The infamous Juan Rubio Latorro, El Bandolero, strikes terror into the hearts of the innocent and bathes the west in blood. He robs and kills with impunity — until he kidnaps the daughter of a powerful rancher and gets man-hunter Wade Rannigan on his trail. But, haunted by his past, Wade becomes reckless and is plagued by mistakes and foolish risks. Can he overcome his own failings and bring Latorro to justice — or will he wind up just another of the deadly El Bandolero's victims?

DATE DUE FOR RETURN

Renewals
www.liverpool.gov.uk/libraries
0151 233 3000

LANCE HOWARD

BANDOLERO

Complete and Unabridged

LINFORD
Leicester

1

The bank window exploded as a body crashed through and slammed into the boardwalk. Shards of glittering glass rained to the ground. The body, a man's, rolled into the dusty street. A scarlet lily blossomed on his chest. He gasped a shuddering liquidy breath and lay still.

Wade Rannigan knew he was too late.

El Bandolero had reached Darkwood and delivered his first victim.

'Jesus H. Christamighty,' Wade whispered, a knot of regret tightening in his gut. If only he'd caught up to the scalawag a few moments earlier things might have been different and Darkwood's widow count wouldn't have increased by one.

He shook his head and stepped out of the saddle before his horse came to a stop. Crouching, he guided the bay to a hitch rail, tethered the animal, then eased a Colt from the holster at his hip.

As Wade edged closer to the bank, a man's shout snapped from inside, stopping him in his tracks. He fought to suppress a surge of apprehension.

Hell, what does it matter, Rannigan? You don't give a damn if that sonofabitch kills you. You ain't got horse spit to live for anyhow.

He shook off the dark thoughts. They would do him little good and he had a mission to complete. If he held one thing above his simmering desire to step off this Godforsaken world it was duty, and by Christ he'd do it.

The bank door burst open and a second shout crashed through the wide main street.

'Anyone who tries following they will get what that *hombre* yonder got, eh?' The man ducked his chin towards the body sprawled in the street as he backed through the door.

Wade brought his Colt up, settling its

aim on the bandit's wide back. A woman's shriek made him hesitate, clench his teeth. The bandit had turned, angling himself away from anyone inside who might take a notion to back-shoot him. With the outlaw's move, Wade glimpsed a swatch of blue flower-print material, and a dark dread made his belly plunge.

The bandit whirled, as if having some sixth sense that Wade was drawing a bead on him, confirming Rannigan's worst fears.

'*Madre del diablo*, who the hell are you, *señor*?' The man's tone carried an icy challenge. The hardcase held a woman in front of him, as a shield. Arm jammed across her throat, a satchel gripped in the same hand, he dragged her backwards across the boardwalk. Her blue flower-print skirt tangled about her legs. Tears streamed from her eyes. The outlaw's free hand gripped a Smith & Wesson, which arced up in a blur, its threatening bore looking like the tunnel straight to hell.

Wade pitched sideways, acting on pure instinct. A shot thundered and the bullet plowed into the boardwalk where he had stood not a second before, burying itself in the wood.

Hitting the planks and executing a shoulder roll, he came up behind a barrel that sat in front of the general store.

A laugh sounded, its tone laced with challenge.

'I do not know who the hell you are, *señor*, but you picked the wrong man to task. I will kill the *señorita* if you try to stop me.'

Wade frowned. 'Give it up, Latorro. You ain't gettin' away. You and me got business.'

A shot answered and lead drilled through the barrel, punching out the opposite side, no more than an inch from Wade's head. Water spouted from the hole, puddling on the boards.

Wade chanced a look, saw the bandit dragging the girl towards an alley. He let out a blistering curse. He'd tracked this fella too far to let him just waltz away, but what could he do? He wouldn't have innocent blood on his hands.

The hardcase hauled her around the corner and Wade straightened, easing forward. From inside the bank came the sounds of muffled activity, a few barked questions, but no one set a foot outside. Wade wondered where the goddamned sheriff had gotten to.

A shot rang out and Wade's belly cinched. With sudden horror he knew what had happened.

'Godamighty . . . ' His whisper died in the echoes of the shot.

A sorrel tore from the alley, skidding around the corner, dust and dirt flying. The bandit let out a whoop, swung his Smith & Wesson and fired a parting shot that sent Wade diving for the cover of a supporting beam. Lead plowed into the general store window, blowing it to smithereens.

Wade jerked up his gun, triggering a shot before he had time to aim. Hitting a moving target was problematic at best, but the bandit, bending low in the saddle, angled left then right and the bullet missed.

Almost.

Wade got lucky. Lead sizzled by the sorrel's left ear, just missing but sending the animal into a panic. The horse jerked up short. The outlaw shouted, raked spurs into the animal's sides, which only caused the beast to become more agitated. It reared, its hoofs beating at the air as it gave out ululating neighs shrill and filled with terror. The hardcase bellowed and yanked the reins, but the horse danced left, skipped right, kicking up great clouds of dust.

The outlaw lost his satchel. It flew into the dusty street, opening, greenbacks wafting to the ground, gold coins clinking. The horse slammed down hard and the hardcase's boot tore from the stirrup. Arms flailing, the man found himself suddenly airborne.

Wade sprang forward, planning to

take full advantage of the situation. Wasn't likely the man would be in any condition to move once he slammed into the rutted street.

The hardcase must have been born with a horseshoe up his saddle, because he somehow hit the ground like a cat and lit off running. He bolted around a corner into another alleyway. The horse, free of its rider, careened down the street, throwing up dirt and dust and heading for parts unknown.

Wade moved forward, using far less caution than he should have.

That goddamned fella's blessed, you best be careful . . .

Why?

Hell, that was a good question. Dying was something he might damn well welcome.

On instinct, he threw himself against a building as a glimpse of gray flashed from the alley — the man's duster-sleeve. It came with an arm attached to a hand aiming a Smith & Wesson and Wade barely got himself out of the way of a bullet. It ricocheted from a supporting beam.

Hell, Rannigan, maybe that death wish ain't so solid after all . . .

He jerked up his Colt, feathered the trigger. The shot roared in his ears. Lead tore a chunk from the corner of the building inches from the hardcase's head but did no other damage.

The outlaw dove back into the alley and Wade went forward, heart thudding. Reaching the opening, he stopped, flattening against a building. Colt pointed skyward, he edged around, expectant, alert.

The alley was empty.

'What the hell . . . '

A sound wrangled his attention and his gaze lifted. He spotted the bandit hurtling up an outside staircase. The hardcase reached the top, which led to the roof of a false-fronted building.

Wade plucked off another shot just as the man disappeared over the edge, missing.

Plunging into the alley, he ran to the

stairway. He took the steps in leaps, heart pounding in his throat, sweat streaking down his face.

Reaching the top, he holstered his weapon, gripped the edge and pulled himself up.

Stupid.

Plain recklessness and a case of churn-headed thinking if ever there was one. Hell, he'd expected the fella to run, not bushwhack him.

He got no time to think on it. A Smith & Wesson clacked against his face and stars exploded before his eyes.

Wade damn near lost his senses and nearly let go of the edge. He had little notion of what made him hang on.

A harsh laugh rang out, mocking and filled with bastard glee. Hands gripped the front of his shirt and hoisted him upward, over the edge. Hurled sideways, he slammed into the surface of the roof with stunning force.

'Hell, *señor*, you got *cojones*, that I will give you. Not so many men would dare come after El Bandolero. But you are not so careful, no?'

Wade struggled to push himself up. He stared through blurry vision at the man looming over him. The hardcase had holstered his gun and a grin half-swallowed his features. Latorro was enjoying this and had total faith in his own superiority. After the clumsy series of moves Wade had executed he damn well couldn't blame the bandit.

The hardcase stepped forward and bent, grabbing two handfuls of Wade's shirt and hauling him to his feet. The man was powerful as a goddamned longhorn, and Wade felt like a rag doll in his grip.

The outlaw didn't throw him this time. He carried Wade backwards and slammed him against the three-foot-high lip that surrounded three sides of the roof.

Latorro's hands wrapped about Wade's throat, forcing his torso backwards, over the edge. Rannigan twisted his head to see the ground two stories below, knowing if he went over he'd break his neck.

That's what you want, Rannigan. Ain't it? Hell, now's your chance.

No, not until he had that rancher's daughter back safe. There would be time to die later.

Wade grasped handfuls of the man's shirt and struggled to keep from going over. The hardcase jammed a palm against Wade's cheek and forced his head backward and down.

Wade's empty green eyes locked with the outlaw's dull gray orbs. For an instant something passed between them, a look that issued challenge and somehow set them on a one-way trail that led straight to hell. It told him it was not time for things to end. It was only the first step of many.

Wade jerked up his knee, burying it in the man's groin. The outlaw gasped and immediately his grip faltered.

Wade shoved forward and up with all his strength. Straightening, he swung a looping uppercut executed with little sense of aim or balance but nonetheless effective. His knuckles collided with the underneath of the man's chin, snapping the outlaw upright and sending him stumbling backwards.

Wade, gasping, staggered forward and set himself for the finishing blow. The hardcase sputtered and coughed, gripping his crotch.

The blow never came. The bandit sprang up like a rattlesnake striking and launched a punch that came with enough power to take Wade's head off.

Instinct taking over, Rannigan jerked his head sideways, but not enough to escape the blow totally. The fist ricocheted from his jaw and sent him stumbling backward to the edge of the roof.

The hardcase lunged, giving Wade little chance to recover. But the man was shaky from the blows to his groin and jaw and mistimed the move enough for Wade to pitch sideways and loop a clumsy roundhouse as the bandit stumbled past. The punch caught Latorro in the temple, sent him dancing forward and left. The bandit threw out both hands, but was too late. He hit the lip of the roof and went over. Wade heard a vicious thud as the fellow's body hit the landing at the top of the stairs.

Latorro had a horseshoe up his saddle for damn sure, Wade told himself again as he went to the edge of the roof and peered over. The hardcase should have plunged to the ground and ended up in a bone orchard, but instead lay sprawled on the landing, eyes staring straight up with a dazed look.

Gasping, he climbed over the lip and dropped to the landing. He plucked the outlaw's Smith & Wesson from its holster and tossed it over the side. A search of the outlaw's person revealed no other weapons, though he discovered two leather bags of chess-pieces in separate duster-pockets. One pouch held white pieces, the other black. Wade reckoned they weren't important so he shoved them back in the coat, then jammed his hands beneath the man's arms.

He was none too gentle about dragging Latorro down the stairs.

Wade hauled the hardcase into the street, then went to his horse and got a length of rope. He bent, looping it about the hardcase's wrists and stepped back, drawing his Colt, waiting. The hardcase groaned.

'Gawddamn, señor, you got more spit in you than I believed.' The hardcase laughed and something about it struck Wade as damned inappropriate.

'What the hell kind of man are you, Latorro?' he asked in a low voice.

The outlaw struggled up into a sitting position and spat a stream of saliva mixed with blood. Their gazes locked and Rannigan felt that sudden sense of stepping on to the trail to hell hit him again.

'I'm the man who's going to kill you, señor.'

Wade ignored him, though he felt

something cold settle in his belly. 'You and me are gonna take us a little trip tomorrow, Latorro. Know a fella right eager to ask you some questions 'bout his daughter. Then I'm gonna make sure you hang till your goddamned head falls off for killin' that woman you dragged from the bank.'

'One of us will never reach the old man, *señor*. I have no doubt which one it will be.' A grin split his face and Wade repressed the urge to kick it clean off his lips.

He went behind the hardcase and gripped the man's bound wrists, then hauled him to his feet. He shoved the Colt's bore into Latorro's back, urging him forward.

The street was filling with townsfolk who peeked from doorways first, then stepped out on to the boardwalks. Men came from the bank, one obviously the manager, who jutted a finger at the hardcase and yelled, 'Hell, that fella's good as hanged now!'

Latorro's gaze settled on the man,

and the manager's face flushed with fear. He scuttled back into the bank and the bandit laughed.

'Gawddamn yellow townsfolk. Not like you, señor. You got cojones, eh?'

Wade frowned. 'So you told me. An' I reckon you'll be swallowin' yours soon enough.'

'Be careful, señor. I am not so good with my temper at times. I'd hate to end the game early.'

Wade shoved the barrel harder into the man's back, forcing him on to the boardwalk on the opposite side of the street. 'That how you see this, Latorro? Some kind of game?'

The man uttered a humorless laugh. 'Why, of course, señor. A game where the winner takes all, no?'

Wade kept his voice level. 'I reckon Alejandro de la Gato won't see it as such.'

'He is a fool, señor. But you are more so.'

'What the hell's that s'posed to mean?'

The hardcase didn't answer.

Wade guided the man to the door of the sheriff's office. 'Open it,' he commanded and the hardcase complied, stepping inside.

A man sat on the floor against the far wall, hands tied behind his back, a bandanna secured in his mouth. Wade now knew why the sheriff hadn't come to help during the robbery.

The lawdog met his gaze and nudged his head toward a nail holding a key-ring. Wade shoved the hardcase into a cell and slammed the door, then holstered his gun and grabbed the keys, locking the cell.

After replacing the ring on the nail, he freed the sheriff.

'Much obliged, stranger.' The lawdog rubbed his jaw and glanced at the hardcase in the cell, who stared back with a mocking smile. 'That the fella causin' all the ruckus?' The sheriff collapsed heavily in the chair behind his desk. A grandfather clock in the corner chimed two.

Wade nodded, then dragged a hard-back chair before the desk and lowered himself into it. 'He's the one. Best have the funeral man go to the alley next to the bank. Reckon he killed a woman he was using as a shield during his escape.'

The sheriff frowned. 'Good enough to stretch his neck come dawn, far as I'm concerned.'

Wade shook his head and reached into a pocket, drew out a folded paper and flipped it open on the desk. 'Be obliged if you'd let me take him come first light.'

'Judas Priest, that's a mite irregular, ain't it? I don't even know who you are.'

'Reckon hanging him without a trial is irregular as well, but that paper will explain it all.'

The sheriff gazed at the sheet, eyes scanning the lines. 'Why, tarnation, you're Wade Rannigan? I've heard of you. You got quite the reputation.'

A twinge of disgust rose in Wade's being. 'Ain't deserved, and it fetches me a passel more trouble than I care for.'

The sheriff's eyes met his; the lawman seemed to be studying him. Wade shifted in the chair, caring little for the scrutiny.

'I reckon you ain't so all-fired eager to avoid trouble, Mr Rannigan.'

Wade frowned. 'Don't catch you, Sheriff.'

The lawdog leaned back. 'Manhunters look for trouble, don't they? Reckon most are near as bad as the fellas they track down.'

'I ain't one of those, Sheriff. If there's a lick of truth about that reputation of mine I reckon it's what they say about me havin' a sense of fair play and justice.'

The sheriff nodded. 'Willin' to wager that's the God's honest, but I'm just as willin' to bet trouble and you ain't mortal enemies.'

Wade's brow furrowed and his unease increased. He was eager to change the subject.

'He the one who trussed you up that

way?' He indicated the hardcase, who sat on the edge of the bunk, watching the proceedings with disdain.

The sheriff shook his head. 'Wish I could tell you who pistol-whipped me but I don't know. I woke up just 'fore you came in.'

Wade's eyes narrowed and a vague suspicion washed through him, one he couldn't put a finger on. Why would a hardcase such as Latorro, a man who placed as much value on life as a rattlesnake did, bother tying up the sheriff instead of killing him?

Wade picked up the paper, folded it and stuffed it back into his pocket. 'You'll let me take him?'

The sheriff sighed, nodded. 'Reckon. De la Gato's a powerful man in Colorado Territory. Has to be to get the governor to throw in with him. From the things I heard about him, though, he ain't a hell of a lot better than that waste of hide you got sittin' in my cell. Can't rightly see a man like yourself workin' for him.'

Wade nodded, knowing the piece of paper in his pocket signed by the governor ordering any lawman to place Latorro in his custody was likely little more than a case of hand-greasin' for some favor a rich man like de la Gato could return during the next election.

'Reckon I ain't so particular who I work for long as the cause is right.'

'What is the cause, Rannigan? Why work for a man like de la Gato when you could take any of a hundred cases across the West?' The sheriff's eyes hardened.

'An innocent gal's life, Sheriff. See, whatever the hell else de la Gato might be, I reckon he loves his daughter. If I got a chance at bringing her back safe it's my duty to try. Latorro took her and I aim to find out where and why.'

A shadow crossed the lawdog's face. 'If she's still alive . . . '

Wade's belly cinched. 'Reckon that's a big if, but he'll hang just as pretty either way.'

The sheriff nodded. 'He's yours.'

Wade glanced at the bandit, who had a bemused look on his face, then stood, sighing. 'I'll be back for him first light, way I said. I'll stop at the telegraph office and file my report with de la Gato, tell him I'm bringin' that scalawag in, then I reckon I'll make me a stop at the saloon and see a gal about a bell.'

The lawdog grinned. 'Ask for Tilly — she rings the sweetest.'

A laugh came from the cell and Wade's gaze shifted to the hardcase. Latorro brought his hands from behind his back, dangling the length of rope Wade had used to bind his wrists. He dropped it on the floor and stood, coming to the cell door and gripping the bars.

'You will never get me to tell you where that gal is, *señor*. You will never make it back to the old man alive.'

Wade wished he could get the gnawing apprehension out of his belly but the outlaw's cockiness was unnerving.

'Reckon you'll damn well tell me or I'll string you up 'fore we get there, Latorro.'

The hardcase reached into his duster and for a moment Wade tensed, worrying that he hadn't searched him well enough. He readied himself for a quick draw.

Latorro eased his hand from the pocket and tossed something on to the floor. It rolled across the boards to stop at Wade's feet. He looked down to see an ivory chess piece, a pawn.

'What the hell?' the sheriff muttered.

Latorro kept his gaze locked on Wade. 'The game's only just started, señor. I have opened the gambit, and sacrificed a pawn. Take it. It is yours. But remember, I still hold my queen and I always win . . . '

Ice trickled through Wade's belly. Some devious intent he couldn't read lay behind the hardcase's dull gray eyes.

'What the hell you mean by that, Latorro?'

The bandit laughed and went back to

the bunk, lay down, hand draped across his forehead.

'I will see you at dawn, *señor*. Do not keep me waiting . . . '

Wade looked to the sheriff, whose face set in grim lines.

'Sure you don't want a couple of deputies?' asked the lawdog.

Wade shook his head. 'I work best alone. Just keep your eyes open tonight. First sign of any trouble, don't hesitate to fill him full of lead.'

'Judas Priest, Rannigan, I don't like this one lick. An' I don't like the look in your eyes.'

Wade turned, went to the door, pausing with his hand on the handle. 'What look might that be, Sheriff?'

The lawdog frowned. 'An empty look. A goddamn empty look.'

2

The morning sun splashed the horizon with shades of scarlet as it peeked above the low hills far in the east. A forest of blue spruce, Douglas fir and Rocky Mountain juniper rose to either side of the hard-packed trail, veined with quaking aspen, canyon maple and cottonwood. Leaves lurid with gold, scarlet and orange flittered in the breeze. Pine scented the brisk air. Ribbons of sunlight the color of blood shivered across the ground.

Depression washed over Wade as he rode along the trail. After visiting the saloon and engaging the services of a soiled dove named Tilly, who, as the sheriff had said, could ring a bell as sweet as any woman versed in the wages of sin, he'd spent most of the night locked in fitful slumber. Despite her skillful ministrations, he had fallen into bed unsatisfied and empty.

You should be used to that by now, Rannigan . . .

For it was always the same; no matter how many doves he enlisted, they were never enough to fill the emptiness in his soul.

He doubted anything could.

Except possibly death.

Refusing to dwell on it, he drew a deep breath and focused on the duty at hand. He needed to deliver Latorro to a pompous windbag named Alejandro de la Gato and discover just what the hardcase had done with or to the man's daughter, Camilla. He reckoned the hardest part was over; he had captured the infamous El Bandolero and while it didn't classify as the easiest case of his career, it hardly qualified as the most difficult, either. Latorro should have proved harder to catch. Could Wade chalk that up to a case of the bandit simply having an overblown reputation? Or was it something more than that?

He shot a glance backwards, gaze

settling on the man walking behind the horse. Latorro cast him a look pregnant with some hidden promise Wade had little desire to see delivered. Upon retrieving the prisoner shortly before dawn, he had substituted wrist-manacles for rope, since the hardcase appeared so adept at freeing himself from bonds. A rope ran from the saddle to the bracelets. Latorro wouldn't have an easy time of it. The journey would take two days at a steady clip, perhaps three or four at a leisurely pace, and El Bandolero would walk every damned step. If he dropped in his tracks from exhaustion, so much the better. Latorro would tell where he had hidden that girl or Wade would let the buzzards have their fill.

Latorro. El Bandolero. A hardcase with an ever-mounting reputation throughout the darkest corners of the West. He didn't look like so much now, walking along behind the horse. But a cynical voice inside told Wade appearances were deceiving.

He swiveled his head forward, cursing himself for his sloppiness where Latorro's capture was concerned. He had achieved his goal despite a series of blunders, any one of which might have cost him his life. He'd made too many mistakes lately. Wasn't much of a stretch to figure out why, either.

Wade Rannigan was a man who courted death. Hell, what did he have to live for? Wormwood days spent missing a woman he'd never gotten the chance at a future with? Empty nights laced with blood-soaked nightmares wherein he was forced to relive each horrifying moment of her death a hundred times over? Some hollow duty?

'Christina . . . ' he whispered, the sound of her voice bitter-sweet on his lips.

Goddammit, why did you have to leave me?

Emotion cinched his throat. His mind wandered and ahead on the trail he swore he saw sunlight swirl into patterns of a woman, arms reaching out, face shimmering with a ghostly aura.

Then the light turned crimson and blood flowed over the vision, streaking down her face and pooling in his soul. He let out a startled gasp and the vision melted, leaving only God-awful emptiness and grief.

Lordamighty, how I miss you . . .

A laugh tore him from his thoughts and at once he felt irritated and relieved. Cranking his head, Wade saw the damnable smugness welded on Latorro's face and his irritation stepped up a notch.

'What the hell's under your saddle?' Wade's voice came sharp, betraying his agitation.

'You are going to die, *señor*. Maybe not today, maybe not tomorrow. But soon, I think.'

Wade sighed. 'Reckon you keep spoutin' off like that I'll have me plenty of company when the time comes.'

The hardcase peered at him. Hatless, beads of sweat speckled his brow, a few trickling down his mustachioed face. Latorro, not a tall man, was built for power, wide and thick across the shoulders. His black hair was a tangled thatch. Wade had studied the hardcase's history before tracking him. The man was a conundrum, a devilish conglomeration of straight desperado and slick inside man. Of mixed blood, Mex and white, he had held up banks and stages, but at the same time was known to hire out to prosperous ranches under the guise of a cowhand, so he could work his way nice and close to a safe or some other treasure he desired. That had been the case with de la Gato, except in this instance the treasure proved to be the man's eighteen-year-old daughter.

Latorro's eyes sparkled with perverted amusement. 'You are not afraid, señor. You are the first *hombre* I meet who is not. Even the old man feared El Bandolero.'

'That ruin your day, Latorro?'

'Makes little difference to me, Señor Rannigan. You will die as any man. But you are not afraid of death, either, are you? I see haunts in your eyes. You have lost the will to live.'

Wade uttered a vapid laugh. 'That oughta make you all the more worried.' Wade turned his head toward the trail.

The laugh came from behind him again and he tensed. His patience with Latorro was as worn as his saddle. He entertained half a notion to string him from the nearest branch and be done with it. If it weren't for de la Gato's daughter he damn well might have.

'*Señor*, my face will burn without a hat.'

The image of that innocent woman being dragged into the alley rose in his mind and any flicker of compassion hardened.

'What'd you do with Camilla de la Gato?' Wade's voice came stony.

'She is a fine woman . . . '

'So you been sayin' since I started askin' you at the jail. You tell me where she is and you'll get your goddamned hat.'

'You are a fool, *señor*. You refuse to see what is right before your eyes.'

'What the hell's that s'posed to mean?' The bandit's taunt annoyed him more than it should have, likely because since capturing Latorro Wade had struggled with a gut feeling that he was missing something. But what?

Why was the sheriff trussed up instead of killed?

Was that it? Why had Latorro left the lawdog alive, then ruthlessly and needlessly murdered that woman during his escape? It made little sense, but maybe it simply fit into the bandit's overall contradictory pattern of operation.

A feeling of being watched invaded his thoughts and he scanned the trail ahead. His gaze swept to either side, searching behind tree and brush for any sign of movement or threat. Nothing. Everything appeared as it should be. The feeling dissolved as fast as it had come and he shook his head.

Latorro ignored the question and let

out a grunt. 'My legs, they begin to cramp, *señor*. I cannot walk such a distance.'

Wade uttered a sharp laugh. 'I'd be right obliged to drag you the rest of the way.'

'You are a hard man, Señor Rannigan. A hard man.' The mockery in the hardcase's voice was enough to make Wade want to back over him with the horse.

★　★　★

The remainder of the day passed in silence, Wade guiding the horse in a monotonous gait along the wooded trail, the hardcase trudging along behind, dark eyes clouded by concealed thoughts.

As he reached a clearing, Wade sent the bay towards a stream that snaked parallel the length of the trail.

The sun dipping into the distant Rockies, dusk invaded the landscape with the suddenness of the Devil

yanking down a shade. Shadows length-
ened into menacing shapes.

Reaching a stand of cottonwoods, he
dismounted, casting a glance at the
hardcase.

A sarcastic smirk turned Latorro's
lips. 'Do we not walk through the night,
señor?'

Wade's gaze narrowed. 'I'm getting
plumb tired of your mouth, Latorro.
You'd best button it 'fore I take a
notion to do just that.'

'It would be healthier for you, señor.
Do not turn your back on me.'

Wade had seen less threatening grins
on skulls.

'Don't fret on it, I ain't plannin' to.
And just in case you got somethin'
planned, you even piss suspicious I
won't hesitate to put lead 'twixt your
peepers. You got that?'

The hardcase scrutinized him. 'I do
believe you, señor. I do believe you. But
I do not give a damn.'

Wade went to the hardcase, untied
the rope from the manacles, then

tethered the bay to a branch. Latorro watched his every move. Wade returned to his prisoner and shoved the outlaw towards a boulder.

'Sit.' His voice left no room for argument.

The hardcase's face didn't change expression as he lowered himself to the ground. 'As you wish, *señor*. My legs, they are almost gone.'

Wade studied him, noting the man appeared far less fatigued than he let on, despite having walked most of the day with little water and no food.

'We'll ride at first light. Reckon I'll have you back and ready for your necktie party in three days or less.'

For the first time a glint of doubt sparked in the hardcase's eyes. Wade wondered if it had started to sink in that the trail they were on led to death, or if perhaps something the hardcase had in mind wasn't falling into place the way he expected it to.

Don't get too sure of yourself, Rannigan. You made a passelful of mistakes already.

Wade went about gathering pieces of branches for a fire, then coaxed an anemic flame into a blaze, the warmth quickly warding off the chill of the encroaching night. Fishing a blue enameled pot from his saddle bags, along with a ration of Arbuckle's beans and jerky, he went to the stream. He filled the pot with water, added the crushed beans and set it to brewing. After unraveling his bedroll, he tossed his hat on to the blanket and lowered himself to the ground beside the fire. He jammed a piece of jerky between his teeth. The first stars appeared, glittering like tiny skulls peering from the velvet shroud of the Colorado sky.

'You treat all your captives this way, *señor*?' The outlaw's voice came as icy as the night promised to be.

Wade eyed him with malice. 'Only the ones who murder innocent women and kidnap ranchers' daughters.'

'You still refuse to open your eyes, Señor Rannigan.'

Wade's brow knotted. 'You got somethin' to say come out and say it, Latorro. I ain't one for games.'

The hardcase leaned back against the boulder. 'The game is everything, *señor*. Everything. Without it there is no reason to exist. But maybe for you there is no reason anyway, eh?'

'Don't get your hopes up, you sonofabitch. I'll get you back to de la Gato and see you swing. You got my word on it.'

No humor came with Latorro's laugh. 'Do you refuse to listen as well as see, *señor*? I told you I will never hang.' The hardcase's face darkened. 'I will not pay for a crime that is not mine.'

'Reckon de la Gato won't see it that way. You best tell me where that gal is.'

'She is not so far, *señor*, not so far.'

Wade felt a twinge of hope. 'You sayin' she's still alive?'

An evasive look crossed Latorro's face. 'I am saying you will find her when the time is right, nothing more.'

Wade tossed the remainder of his

jerky into the fire, disgust for the bandit ruining his appetite. 'Why didn't you kill that lawdog in Darkwood?'

Latorro smiled and looked at the ground, then back up. 'Surely you would not deprive me of an evening meal, *señor*?'

Wade saw resolution set in the outlaw's dark eyes. He would answer nothing further.

More annoyed than ever, Wade reached into a saddlebag and pulled out a hardtack biscuit. It was crawling with maggots. He tossed it into the sand at Latorro's feet.

'Reckon that oughta hold ya.'

Latorro's face darkened, for the first time irritation glinting behind his eyes. 'You will die suffering for that, *señor*.'

'Way you got it figured, I'm gonna die anyway. What the hell difference does it make?'

'It makes all the difference in the world, Señor Rannigan. Some men, they go quick, way that lady I killed at the bank went. She had done nothing to me, so I showed her mercy. But you should have seen her brains come out her ear, eh? It was a sight to savor.'

Disgust clutched in Wade's belly. 'You're a goddamned gruesome sonofabitch, Latorro.'

'I enjoy killing, *señor*, much the way you do.'

Wade let out a scoffing sound. 'How you got that figured?'

'Would you not enjoy putting a bullet through my brains, *señor*? Would you not enjoy watching me hang? We are not so different, you and I, eh?'

Suddenly uneasy, Wade rose to his feet. 'We're a hell of a lot different, way I see it. You kill for the sheer pleasure of it. I kill for duty.'

The outlaw laughed a mocking laugh. 'And what else, *señor*? To erase the haunts in your eyes, no? To chase away the emptiness you live with?'

Wade averted his gaze, emotion tightening his throat. Christ, that fella got under his skin. He was used to bringing in hardcases quickly, stringing them up or putting lead betw___ ___ ___ir eyes, not debating philosophies with them. Perhaps prolonging this was proving to be another mistake, but he'd been determined to make the hardcase tell what he had done with de la Gato's daughter.

'You got it all wrong, Latorro. I just make sure the West is safe from men like you. Don't matter to me whether they come in dead or alive, but the killin' ain't the enjoyable part. The satisfaction of knowing I might have saved some innocent life is.'

'Look in the mirror, señor. Look deep into it and tell me then you don't see me peering back at you. We are much alike. Killing is in our blood. It is a fever we cannot escape. And soon I will see your blood soak the ground, señor. I always win.'

The hardcase snatched up the hardtack biscuit and bit off a huge chunk, maggots and all. He ate in silence, staring at the ground. Wade felt nausea twist in his belly and turned away, watching the hardcase from the corner of his eye, while looking out at the stream.

The water burbled along, tumbling over rocks, sprinkled with dancing reflections of starlight.

A gnawing guilt washed over him. Was the hardcase right? Were they alike? What did Wade see when he looked in the mirror? A man who hunted down others and brought them to swift justice — or a killer?

No. He was no killer. He never felt elation at the death of another, only a sense of duty fulfilled and grim justice.

Killing was a game to El Bandolero, one he played to win. Perhaps in ways he refused to admit, Wade did as well. If that weren't the case wouldn't a bullet have found him years ago, soon after Christina's death?

Sorrow drifted over him and his gaze riveted upon the rippling waters, seeking out the patterns of moonlight wavering within. Her face formed, soft features beckoning, eyes beseeching.

41

'Christina . . . ' he whispered.

You cannot die . . .

Her voice? A memory?

Perhaps only the wind.

A biting agony at his throat shattered his reverie. He gasped.

'I told you not to turn your back on me, señor,' came a grating voice in his ears. Silent as a night cat, the hardcase had risen to his feet and gotten his manacled hands over Wade's head and around his throat. The links pressed deep into his flesh, cutting off his air and sending sparkles of light across his vision. Wade frantically clutched at the chain, struggling to pry the links away from his Adam's apple. A low buzz swarmed through his mind and his lungs began to ache.

He kicked out, fighting to break free, boot heels skidding on the hard-packed ground. The scenery around him blurred. Latorro laughed behind him.

'The game is finished, señor. You are no player, eh?'

Perhaps it was a flashing notion he

still had a duty to complete or perhaps it was Latorro's ridicule, but something ignited whatever bastard spark of life that drove him to cling to this world. Wade tried to throw himself right, then left, struggling furiously to loosen the chain across his throat as his fingers pried between flesh and metal. He snapped a backward kick, raking the bandit's shin.

The hardcase let out a roar and swung Wade back and forth. Deprived of air, his lungs burned and pain splintered across his chest. He felt weakness invade his legs, his strength fading.

With every remaining ounce of strength, he threw himself backward. The outlaw had been prepared for him to struggle or even fall forward, the way most men reacted when caught from behind. The move took Latorro off guard enough to send him shuffling a handful of steps backwards.

The hardcase stumbled into the camp-fire and bellowed. He stamped about in the flames, suddenly more concerned with burning than with holding on to Wade.

Acting more from instinct than skill, Wade twisted as the chain slackened. Turning himself towards the bandit, he brought a fist up in a crisp arc in the same move. The blow thudded against Latorro's ribs and the hardcase grunted, cursed. Flames danced around them, sparks singeing their trousers and hair.

Wade jerked free of the bandit's grip, ducking down and under the man's encircling arms, then lurching sideways out of the flames.

Latorro danced backwards, slapping at snakes of flame on his trousers. Wade, gasping, fought to clear his vision. He recovered sight just enough to see the bandit's blurry form lunge at him again, fist raised for a hammering blow.

Wade, throwing himself sideways, barely got out of the way in time. He hit the ground, landing hard on a branch he had intended to use in the camp-fire later. His fingers curled around its thick base, and he spun, coming half-way to his feet as Latorro leaped at him.

Wade swung the branch in a crisp arc. Wood clacked off the hardcase's thick forehead with the sound of a mallet slamming into a rail post. Latorro dropped in his tracks.

Wade tossed aside the branch and stood, panting, agony tearing at his throat.

You were goddamn lucky that time, Rannigan. You should be dead. Another mistake like that and you will be.

In a burst of self-disgust, Wade delivered a kick to the hardcase's ribs. It felt wholly satisfying, but he couldn't figure who he was more peeled with, himself or Latorro.

The outlaw groaned and muttered, 'Bastard.' His dark eyes locked on Wade. 'You are a hard man to kill for someone who wants to die so bad, señor . . .'

'Told you you had me figured wrong,

Latorro.' Rannigan's words came through gasped breaths, voice raspy. 'You're my duty, now. I aim to see it through. Reckon it's my game from here on out.'

The hardcase's fingers went to the welt on his forehead. Anger flashed in his eyes, dark promise.

'It is the Devil's game, *señor*. The next move will belong to me and I will play my queen.'

Wade stumbled to his horse, pulling a Winchester from the saddle boot. Latorro crawled back to his spot by the boulder, nursing his ribs.

Wade got a sudden stabbing regret that he hadn't brought another horse and returned this man to de la Gato as quickly as possible. He had misjudged Latorro. The outlaw would not be broken. He was a scorpion of a man and Wade wondered if even stretching his neck would kill him.

He lowered himself to his blanket beside the fire and locked his gaze and the Winchester barrel on the hardcase.

He remained awake the entire night.

3

As false dawn washed the horizon in shades of gray, Wade stretched and went to his horse, shoving the Winchester into the saddle boot. Frost-coated fallen leaves crackled beneath his boots. The night had been cold, but no colder than the feeling in his soul. With plenty of time to dwell on mistakes and second-guess himself, his mood had only deteriorated. Latorro, unperturbed by his predicament, had fallen fast asleep. Wade's throat ached powerfully and his fingers went to his Adam's apple, massaging. He'd been damned lucky the bandit hadn't killed him, though he wondered if luck had much to do with it. The hardcase's words haunted him: for a man with a death-wish he made a hell of an effort at staying alive.

Annoyed, he walked over and kicked Latorro with gusto in the ribs, rousing him.

'You snore like a sonofabitch.' Wade stooped and secured the rope around the manacles then hitched it to his saddle after untethering his bay and leading it near the hardcase.

'I must piss, *señor*.' Latorro's voice came tinged with irritation.

'Then do it in your goddamned trousers, 'cause after that stunt you pulled last night I ain't leavin' you be for even a second.'

Wade went to his horse and stepped into the saddle. He glanced back to the hardcase, who cast him a glare. 'You best get on your feet or I'll drag your carcass all the way to hell.'

The hardcase spat and clumsily gained his legs.

'You'll pay for this, Señor Rannigan.' Spite laced the man's voice now; no longer did it carry the cockiness of the day before.

With a humorless chuckle, Wade

heeled the horse into an easy walk on to the trail.

The sun climbed higher and frost melted, dripping like liquid diamonds from leaves. A musky sweet-sour odor of decay scented the air. He shot occasional glances at Latorro; the man remained oddly silent, face locked in an unreadable mask. Perhaps his situation was sinking in, and Wade had made the right choice after all.

Don't get too confident, he warned himself. He knew from experience that sometimes things went the most tranquil right before the explosion.

With the notion, Wade tensed, the sudden feeling of being watched stalking him again. His gaze swept the trail ahead, but he spotted nothing out of the ordinary. Although everything appeared peaceful, he found himself unable to shake the feeling.

Was someone keeping track of their progress, following them? By all accounts, Latorro worked alone, except for rumors of a partner in the bandit's early days.

The feeling dissolved as rapidly as it had come, though it left suspicion simmering in his belly. Like a saddle that didn't quite fit, it rubbed him the wrong way.

The woodland thinned, giving way to open stretches clustered with stands of trees; low hills rose far to his left, littered with boulders, studded with brush.

The day wore on, cool, though the sun shined with an intensity that only came with autumn in these parts. He cast a glance backward at Latorro, noting the man's face twisted with spite now.

'Gettin' tired of the game, Latorro?' Wade's voice held a certain measure of mockery but he reckoned his heart wasn't in it.

'You are making a big mistake, *señor*. You cannot win.'

'Looks like I'm holdin' my own so far.'

'Hell is filled with men who held

their own, *señor*.'

The miles trickled away. Latorro began to stumble and Wade doubted it was an act. Any other man would have dropped by now.

'You ready to tell me where that gal is yet, Latorro?' he shouted over his shoulder.

'The queen will soon be ready to play, *señor*. If you are a righteous man you should make your peace with your God now.'

'Goddammit, I wish you'd stop talkin' in riddles and make this easier on all concerned.'

'You mean make it easier to hang me . . . ' The bandit's tone turned colder, certain.

That, too, Wade thought, but said, 'Reckon if she's alive you might get a fair trial. Leastwise I'll put in a word for you.' Although it would gall him, he would hold to his word. If the hardcase told him where Camilla de la Gato — or her body — was hidden, he would see to it Latorro got a trial instead of letting the rancher hang him.

'I am truly touched, *señor*.' The mocking returned to the hardcase's voice. 'You are a man of honor, but I can tell you nothing your eyes do not already see . . . '

Wade let out a sigh, the notion that he was missing something right in front of him plaguing his thoughts again.

The woodland opened further and the day waned. The sun dipped towards the mountains and Wade reckoned only a couple hours daylight remained. It struck him that the area was far too open for his tastes. If someone were indeed dogging him, he would be exposed to attack from the flanking hillside. If he didn't make camp now it would only get worse. The low hills and stream would give way to rolling grassland and distant mountains within a handful of miles.

Latorro works alone . . .

The thought invaded his mind again and along with it came doubt. What if someone *were* aiding the outlaw? What if Latorro had broken routine? What wasn't Wade seeing? His gaze lifted to the low hills, searching for any sign of movement or glinting metal, but the angle was wrong. Everything sparkled like diamonds, likely chips of mica or feldspar within the boulders, glittering with sunlight.

The sheriff wasn't killed . . .

Had someone else tied up the lawdog while Latorro hit the bank then run at the first sign of trouble?

Wade angled the horse to the right, reining up beside a stand of cotton-woods paralleling the stream. The ground, littered with rocks and a large deadfall, sloped toward the water.

He tethered the bay to the limb, from the corner of his eye observing Latorro. The hardcase cast a furtive glance at the hills, as if searching for something and Wade felt another prickle of apprehension. The more he thought it over the more certain he became that El Bandolero had changed tactics and had someone working with him, someone keeping a distance, waiting for an opportunity to strike.

He turned to Latorro. 'First sign of trouble I'll put a bullet in your skull. You best keep that in mind.'

Latorro let a grin oil his lips then sat heavily beside the deadfall. 'We shall see, *señor*. We shall see.'

Wade scanned the hills again and saw only sunlight glinting off rock. The stalked feeling returned, but until something happened he could do little about it except keep a watchful eye.

He yanked his Winchester from the saddle boot, then set about gathering up branches to build a fire.

'Reckon we'll make de la Gato's late tomorrow.' Wade set a coffee-pot next to the flames. 'You got any notion of tellin' where that gal is you best do it 'fore we get there. That old man ain't likely to be as forgivin' as I am.'

A shadow crossed Latorro's hard features. 'I know all about de la Gato, *señor*. He is an arrogant sonofabitch who has too much for any one man.

He has no honor.'

Wade almost laughed, but the hardcase's voice carried a note of deadly seriousness.

'An' I s'pose you do?'

'I am an honorable man in my way, *señor*. When I steal and kill I make no attempt to deny it and I play by the rules I set. De la Gato would have men believe he is something he is not. He does not love his daughter, *señor*. He is driven to possess her, much the way he possesses his cattle. He orders her to marry the son of the governor, forge an alliance between them, one that will make them richer men than they are already. His motives are no different than mine, Señor Rannigan.'

'You sayin' he wants his daughter back because of greed?'

Latorro nodded. 'Now you see, *señor*.'

Wade let out a scoffing grunt. 'Find that hard to believe, even from a pompous old windbag like de la Gato.'

The outlaw's eyes narrowed. 'His

masquerade is everything to him, *señor*. How would it look for him to lose his daughter to a bandit? He would be a fool in the eyes of those he seeks to impress. To have all he has gained mocked would make him a laughing-stock, would it not?'

Wade shrugged. 'You don't rightly impress me as a fella to care one way or the other.'

'You are right, *señor*. I do not care. Let him have his foolish deception. He is alive for one reason alone.'

'What might that be?' Wade's eyes narrowed, something in the man's words disturbing him for no reason he could pinpoint. De la Gato was a greedy sonofabitch, a callous, arrogant man, but Wade had a hard time believing he didn't love his daughter. Despite that, he reckoned Latorro had little reason to lie on that account.

'That is no business of yours, *señor*.'

Wade stared at him, puzzled. 'Reckon you got it wrong, Latorro. Governor signed a paper turnin' you over to me.

Folks know you kidnapped that man's daughter and that'll do nothing but elicit sympathy and further his cause.'

Latorro shook his head. 'You have closed your ears, *señor*.'

'De la Gato paid you the ransom you asked for. Why didn't you just give her back then or tell him you killed her? Since you see yourself as such an honorable man, seems like that'd be the fair thing to do.'

'Pull your head from the sand, *señor*. I was robbing a bank when you caught me. Why would I do such a thing so soon if I had been given this money as de la Gato claims?'

'Maybe you're just more greedy than the old man.'

'*Madre del Diablo*, that I am, but I am not stupid.'

'Hell, I might be inclined to debate that with you if I gave a goddamn.'

'You are as foolish as the old man, *señor*. The game will end the same for you both. With death.'

Wade's fingers tightened on the

Winchester. 'You'll hang when we get there. I'll see to it personally 'less you tell me where that man's daughter is.'

A confident expression crossed the outlaw's face. His gaze shifted to the low hills. 'I believe you will have your answer in a moment, *señor*. The game is over. And I still hold the queen.'

'What the goddamn hell are you talkin' . . . ' A plunging sensation hit Wade's belly and he stiffened, gaze lifting to the distance. He brought the Winchester up as he caught a glimpse of waning sunlight flashing off gun-metal close to a boulder.

'Jesus . . . ' Wade whispered, knowing he was too late.

A shot blasted, echoing across the countryside like demons laughing.

Lead punched into Wade's left shoulder and kicked him backwards. The Winchester flew from his grip and he slammed into the ground on his back, breath exploding from his lungs. Blurred light and dark streaks criss-crossed his vision. Burning agony radiated across his shoulder and blood streamed down beneath his arm to soak into the soil.

A harsh laugh sounded, grating yet muffled in his ears as his consciousness wavered. He was barely aware of the hardcase standing over him, peering down. From the distance rose the crescendoing rhythm of approaching hoofbeats. It came to a sudden stop.

'You took your time getting here!' he heard Latorro bellow.

'Keep your britches on, you sonofa-bitch!' A woman's voice. 'Had to wait till he got out into the open, didn't I?'

'You let it go too long . . . ' The outlaw's voice came with bitterness.

Wade couldn't see the woman's face; she stayed back between the outlaw and a horse, but he heard cottony sounds of movement.

'We best finish him off and get goin'.' The woman's voice held no more compassion or mercy than Latorro's.

Dread surged over him. Christ, he'd prayed for death countless times over the past years, prayed for an end to the pain and emptiness he'd been forced to live and now it was here. It galled him that it would be Latorro who released him and that he wouldn't complete his mission. From somewhere hidden inside came a will to fight the inevitable, but he couldn't force himself to move. Stunned, he was paralyzed where he lay. His senses were threatening to desert him and his life's blood was pouring down his side. He had no chance, and still he held on. In that moment before death it struck him with spite that he had more of the game in him than he wanted to admit.

Through blurred vision he saw a dark shape hover closer. Focusing, he watched the shape fuse into the outlines of the outlaw's gloating face.

'Like I said, I have the queen, *señor*. You should have listened more closely, eh?' The outlaw squatted and plucked the Colt from Wade's holster, holding it in his manacled hands.

'Latorro . . . ' Wade whispered, 'you

best make sure you do the job of killin'
me right, you son . . . of . . . a
bitch . . . '

'I had truly hoped for more of a
challenge, Señor Rannigan. I expected
better from you. You disappoint me.'

A second shot rang out and the
hardcase jerked straight up, twisting to
look behind him. A shriek came from
the woman poised near the horse.

'Christ, Juan, someone's a-shootin' at
us!' The woman leaped behind the
horse, shielding herself from gunfire.

'What the hell . . . ' The hardcase's
gaze lifted to the hills, eyes narrowing
to a squint.

Another shot followed, kicking up a
chunk of soil inches from Latorro's
boots.

'Kill him and let's get outta here!'
The girl's voice rose to a shrill pitch.
Wade caught a flash of blue clothing as
she swung into the saddle of her horse,
glimpsed the back of her ebony-maned
head.

Latorro glanced at Wade.

'He's good as dead . . . ' the hardcase yelled back to the girl, then, in a lower voice, added: 'You are a dead man, Señor Rannigan, but I will not finish you. I will leave you to the buzzards for what you did to me. They will peck your eyes out and tear the flesh from your face piece by piece. I could do no better than that. I win, *señor*. I win.'

The hardcase shoved the Colt into his own holster, then reached into a pocket of his duster. He brought out a small leather bag tied with a hide drawstring and pulled it open. Turning it upside down, he dumped a stream of white chess pieces atop Wade's chest.

'Checkmate, *señor*.'

He laughed and moved away. He stooped and picked up Wade's rifle, hurling it into the stream. Going to Wade's horse, Latorro untethered the bay and swung into the saddle. Reining around, he let out a 'Yah!' and sent the mount into a gallop just as a third shot rang out, plowing into the ground a few feet from the animal's retreating hoofs.

The woman was in motion an instant behind the outlaw.

Wade lay there, gaze thrown up to the darkening cobalt sky, a soft thrumming swelling in his brain. The pain was starting to fade and that was a goddamn bad sign. Death was closing in.

'Christina . . . ' His whisper melted into the wind.

Time dragged and he couldn't have told how much passed.

A sound.

Hoofbeats. Drawing closer.

Had the outlaw come back to finish him?

The hoofbeats slowed, stopped, and he heard the creak of saddle leather then cautious, approaching steps.

A face loomed above him, peering down, brow etched with concern and a measure of trepidation. At first he mistook it for some sort of angel with chestnut-colored hair tumbling from beneath a Stetson and grim but lovely features. Then he saw the angel aiming a rifle at his chest and he knew he was wrong. He'd never been a God-fearing man and the innards of a church were as alien to him as a sense of contentment, but something told him angels didn't carry Winchesters.

'Who the hell are you?' The woman levered a shell into the chamber to punctuate her words.

4

'I asked you a question, mister.' The girl jabbed the rifle at Wade's chest and her eyes narrowed to slits.

'My name's . . . Rannigan, Wade Rannigan . . . ' His words trickled out and he found himself struggling to cling to consciousness. A flicker of confusion shown in her mahogany-colored eyes. Under any other circumstances, she would have been lovely in a tomboyish sort of way. She pushed her hat from her head, letting it hang by its strap at her back. Chestnut hair, pulled tightly back, wisps corkscrewing to either side of her face, framed a high forehead. Although dressed like a man, her blue denim bib shirt did little to hide the fullness of her breasts, and trousers couldn't disguise the easy flare of her hips.

'The famous bounty hunter?' She

maintained her aim on the rifle but her face lost a notch of its tenseness.

'One and only . . . ' he said, almost a whisper. 'Who are you?'

She shot a glance in the direction Latorro had taken, then looked back to him, disgust on her face. 'Name's Charity Parker, but I reckon that won't mean nothin' to you. Doesn't to no one anymore, but it damn well will to that fella you let get away.'

Irritation pierced the cotton clouding his brain.

'Hell, you're the one who missed hittin' him. You were a better shot we wouldn't be having this conversation.' The outburst took most of his remaining strength and he coughed, the movement sending spasms of pain across his shoulder and chest.

She uttered a derisive grunt. 'Tarnation, you weren't lyin' here with your life's blood pourin' outta ya we wouldn't be neither. I'd be skinnin' his lowly hide right now.'

'Why you after him?' Blackness crept

into the corners of his mind, and he struggled to hold it off. If he gave in he reckoned he'd never see the light of day again. Once more Latorro's words about him being hard to kill for a man with a death-wish came back to him in mocking chorus.

'That ain't no business of yours. An' while we're sittin' here jawin' you'll breathe your last if I don't do somethin' 'bout it. Reckon he got away by now anyhow. I still got me half a mind to leave you and go after him.' She gave him a disgusted look but her tone said different. Beneath her hard exterior Charity Parker had a spark of compassion, though he half wished she would just ride off and let him die in peace.

Without another word, the girl spun and went to her horse, jamming the Winchester into a saddle boot. She returned and shoved both her hands beneath his arms. An explosion of pain splintered all the way across his chest and back. He let out a grunt.

'Hell, Rannigan, this ain't gonna feel

too goddamned good but I need to get you over near the fire.'

She began dragging him over the ground and sweat sprang out on his forehead. She was a hell of a lot stronger than she looked and made quick work of it.

'You cuss like a drover,' he mumbled, trying to keep his mind off the agony. He heard her let out a harsh laugh.

'Reckon you won't find many folk who'd call me much of a lady anyhow, not no more anyway.'

She left him near the fire, then went back to her horse and untied her bedroll. Bringing it to him, she unraveled it and spent the next five minutes making him as comfortable as possible. Sweat and blood soaked him. He had no idea how he remained conscious and cursed himself for doing so. Dying would be far easier, he reckoned.

When she left him for a few moments, his senses began to waver in and out. Before his fading vision, her movements became jerky, snatches of images mixed with swirls of blackness and muffled sounds.

Charity Parker strode to her horse a third time. She removed her saddle-bags and set them beside him, then scooched. He felt her pulling at his shirt, snapping the buttons free, and peeling shreds of cloth away from his wound. He groaned but the pain seemed duller now, further away.

'Jesus H. Christmas . . . ' A measure of worry hung in her voice. 'You're bleeding like a stuck pig and I reckon the bullet's still in ya. Best it comes out.'

He nodded, swallowing hard. She opened her saddle-bags, pulling out a bottle of Orchard, half empty, and removing the top. She set the bottle to his lips and he took a deep pull, a portion of the amber liquid spilling down the side of his face. It burned in his throat and settled warmly in his belly. She set the bottle on the ground.

Sliding a Bowie knife from a sheath

at her waist, she peered at him with a serious expression. 'Reckon I ain't gonna tell you this will feel like Saturday night at the saloon, Rannigan. But I'll do my best not to make it any worse than possible.'

'You done this before?' His words came raspy, barely audible.

'Shore, thousand times over . . . ' She was lying and a note of sarcasm came with it. 'What the hell's the tale with them chess-pieces, anyhow?' As she spoke, she undid the bandanna from around her neck and dabbed at the blood oozing from the wound.

'Latorro figures everything's some kind of game. Kept sayin' he had the queen.'

'Reckon I know as much about chess as I do 'bout diggin' out bullets, but if I recollect right the queen moves the most ways and protects the king. Looks like that gal he's got with him served her purpose well.' She slid the knife-blade into the flames, heating it until it glowed red.

'Please . . . ' he whispered. 'Let me die . . . '

You cannot die . . .

Christina . . .

Charity gazed at him with confusion on her features. 'Are you plumb loco? You mussed up my chance at gettin' that sonofabitch. Least you can do is pull through and help fix that.'

She yanked a cloth from her gear, then leaned towards him and shoved it into his mouth. He bit down, bracing himself. Without ceremony, Charity pressed the tip of the red-hot blade into the wound. He let out a muffled yell and his body went rigid with pain. She probed with the blade, gritting her teeth and narrowing her eyes. As she dug the bullet from his shoulder, he felt numbness swarm over his body, senses a-swim in an ever-thickening sea of blackness. Was this how it felt to die? That was what he wanted, wasn't it? Longed for?

'Hold on, you sonofabitch!' Charity's voice barely penetrated his fading senses. 'Don't you die on me now. I ain't lost a man yet and you ain't gonna be the first.' Her face cinched with determination.

He spat out the cloth, tongue dry and throat parched. 'How . . . how many you tried this on . . . ?' he managed to get out.

'You're the first, Rannigan.' With a skillful motion of the blade tip, she pried the bullet free. It landed in the soil beside him. She set the knife aside, then grabbed the Orchard bottle and poured it over the area. Pain tore through the numbness and he let out a shriek of agony.

For long moments, she worked over him. Fishing in her saddle-bags again, she brought out a box of Winchester cartridges and selected one. Prying the bullet free with her teeth, she dumped the powder on to a swatch of his shirt that she cut away, then with the Bowie knife scraped lint from the blanket, adding it to the powder. A moment later she flipped the swatch on to the wound, applying pressure.

The last thing in his head was she knew what she was doing after all, using the gunpowder remedy to stanch the flow from the wound. Beyond that, his mind wandered in and out of consciousness, flashes of agonizing pain mixing with muffled words from her that he couldn't distinguish.

He wasn't sure whether he blacked out completely or if night had engulfed the camp. A whirl of fevered images tumbled through his mind, taunting, terrifying. The outlaw's grinning face hovered above him, the mocking laugh ringing in his ears.

I still have the queen, señor . . . she belongs to me. You and the old man are fools . . .

'Bastard . . . ' he mumbled and at once he was back in Darkwood, standing outside the bank. The man's body came crashing through the window and he saw the outlaw backing out the door, turning towards him. Only this time the woman locked in his arms was Christina, his sweet Christina, her face twisted with terror, lips mouthing a silent plea for help. But he couldn't help, couldn't save her. He hadn't been able to, all those years ago, and he couldn't now. The outlaw dragged her into the street.

'See, señor? I have her now. She belongs to me. I have won again.' Latorro placed the gun to her head and jerked the trigger. With a flash of gunpowder and acrid blue smoke the world turned upside down. Christina's body crumpled lifelessly to the ground, her blood pooling in the dust. As he stared at her twisted form, she vanished into memory.

Wade took a step towards the man, but Latorro seemed to shrink back until he stood at the far end of the main street. Anger seething through his being, Wade began to run towards him, arm thrust out, hand reaching, fingers splayed.

'Noooo!' he yelled, the sound muffled and dragging. His legs pumped harder but he lost ground, caught in a dream river that made his every step agonizingly slow. Around him the buildings became distorted, nightmarish. Shadows came to life, black fingers reaching for him. His bootfalls reverberated like gunshots.

'I have the queen, Señor Rannigan. I always win . . . ' Latorro's voice faded and his figure vanished as the town melted away.

Blackness.

All around him, swirling clouds of ebony streaked with light from some indistinct source.

'Christamighty . . . ' he whispered. He peered at his shoulder, but saw no wound, felt no pain.

'You must go on, Wade . . . '

Her voice came from behind him. He whirled and she was there, bathed in a shimmering white aura. Christina. Her soft features glowed, radiant and kind, the way he recollected them. Soft brown curls framed her delicate face and compassion and warmth showed in her green eyes. A flowing white gown rippled about the soft curves of her body, the gown he recalled burying her in.

'Am I dead?' he asked in a whisper.

'You must go on, Wade,' she repeated, a smile touching her full lips. He wanted to go to her, hold her in his arms, be with her for eternity, but he couldn't move. He seemed frozen where he stood.

'I want to be with you again . . . please let me.'

'You have the will to live, my love. Go on and finish what you must.'

'I have nothing without you, Christina. I knew that the day . . . ' His words faltered, a great sorrow burning in his heart.

She smiled a warm smile 'You could not have prevented what happened. No one could have. Please accept that. She needs you now. Be with her. She is alone and lost, the same as you.' Her image melted and he struggled to move, unsuccessful. His arm came up, reaching for her as she vanished but his fingers clutched only emptiness. She was gone and he was alone. Again. And he wondered with overwhelming bitterness why death should be any different from life for a man like Wade Rannigan.

'Christinaaa . . . ' His scream faded into nothingness as blackness swept in from all around him and in an instant he was aware of nothing more.

★   ★   ★

Christ on a crutch, things had shorely gone straight to hell, Charity Parker thought with bitterness, as she straightened after fashioning the remains of Wade Rannigan's shirt into a sling. She had done the best she could and if he lived it was because he wanted to — *needed* to. She reckoned that just might be a problem.

She turned and stared off in the direction the hardcase and his woman had taken, and cursed. She had been trailing that sonofabitch for six months and she'd damn near had his sorry hide today. She reckoned she couldn't quite blame his getting away on Rannigan the way she would have liked, because if she'd had half an aim she would have nailed the hardcase with her Winchester instead of wasting three shots on the ground. But she hadn't gotten him, and if there was one thing her brother hadn't taught her well it was how to shoot a goddamn rifle. Tarnation, she could blow a rowdy cowboy's jewels clean out of their crown with an over-and-under, but she was downright lousy with a Winchester. If she had anyone to blame for that scalawag getting away it was herself.

'Sonofabitch,' she muttered. Now what was she gonna do? She turned and looked to the man lying beside the fire. If he recovered it would take a spell for him to mend and be strong enough to ride; by that time Lord knew where Latorro would be.

A surge of hatred rushed through her veins as she dwelled on the outlaw, a hatred she had never felt for any man until Juan Rubio Latorro came along and stole what goddamn little she considered a life. She reckoned she never owned much, but what that fella took was gold to her and though she knew she'd never get it back, she damn sure would make him suffer for taking it.

Hell, you know you'll take him out quicklike.

She sighed, shaking her head. Angry as she was she didn't think deep down that she could find it in herself to prolong even an outlaw's agony. She cursed herself for not being colder, but she reckoned if her brother hadn't taught her to shoot he had damn sure instilled a measure of human compassion in her rawhide soul. What a world it might have been had others chosen to show her the same. She couldn't recollect the last time anyone had offered a helping hand, least not a sincere one that came free and clear of all recompense.

She had her pride, that she did. Folks wouldn't see it as much, given what she done in her life, but it was the last shred of what she might have been that she could lay claim to. And with that pride came loyalty to the one person who had accepted her for what she was and asked nothing in return: her brother.

She would find Latorro and kill him, that was for certain. The Lord would share His vengeance.

What happens after that? The notion struck her unbidden and a sudden welling of sorrow and pain filled her heart. She forced back a tear and clutched her arms about herself. What lay beyond revenge? What was there for a woman such as she, a woman the West would have seen as nothing more than a commodity? Not a goddamn hell of a lot, she reckoned. Not a hell of a lot.

Times a-many she wished things had turned out different, that she had grown into a fashionable upstanding woman who hosted socials and sang in a choir on Sunday mornings. Funny, she shouldn't have even given a damn about that anymore, but whatever else the West had taken out of her it hadn't taken all of her dreams.

'You're a bigger fool than you think!' she chastised herself, shaking her head. 'What call you got even thinkin' on that?'

Her gaze settled on the man lying beneath the blanket. He was responsible for such notions, though the thought struck her as even more foolish than blaming him for Latorro's escape. She took a step closer to him, watched his fluttering eyelids, and it occurred to her that he was an entirely handsome man, even with the sweat streaming down his face. But it was more than looks; there was some deeper attraction she couldn't put words to.

She had heard of Wade Rannigan. Tarnation, not many a man, or woman, hadn't. He was practically a legend in them pulp novels she had seen her brother reading. A manhunter. A professional killer with a sense of honor, a lightning-fast gun, and a reckless courage that made him confront death with iron nerves. Was that all there was to him?

She doubted it. Hell, those books were likely all a pack of lies anyway. Because what they failed to record was that Wade Rannigan was a man looking to die. She had seen it reflected plain in his eyes, would have known even if he hadn't begged her to let him pass.

She peered at him as a groan escaped his lips. He tossed and turned, limbs jerking occasionally, and concluded he was delirious. She wondered what terrors his nightmares held. What haunted a man like Wade Rannigan so much it made him want to die? She found herself strangely eager to find out and for the first time in six months she felt something besides revenge burning in her soul.

She took steps closer to him,

debating whether she should pray, wondering if her Maker would refuse to listen after the life she had led. Hell, what was there to lose? She mouthed a silent supplication that he would pull through and ride with her after Latorro.

You're a fool if you think a man like that would have any interest in a gal like you other than what's bought and paid for, a cynical voice inside taunted. She let out a humorless laugh, perplexed and annoyed at the sudden confused feelings coming over her. Wasn't like her a lick. She was usually all business.

He muttered something in his fever and her ears pricked but she couldn't quite catch it. She moved closer but he suddenly accommodated her curiosity and screamed it out. A name and she felt an odd quiver of jealousy for no reason she could figure. *Christina.* Who was she? And why did he want to die if he had her?

Around her the night closed in and

she shivered. Stars glittered like ice-chips in a cruel indigo sky and the moon cast a ghostly glow over the stream's bubbling waters.

She went to her saddle-bags and brought out a wrapped bundle, opening it to reveal a measure of sassafras bark. She grabbed the coffee pot she had found by the fire and went to the stream, filled it with water, then returned to the bundle. She placed some of the bark into the water and rolled the rest back up, stuffing it into her bags. The aroma of vanilla and orange touched her nostrils as she set the mixture to boiling, brewing a tea that would help alleviate Rannigan's fever. When it was ready, she forced sips of it down his throat, spilling more than she got down.

Cold sweat drenched his body. He started to shake with the chills, despite the warmth of the fire and blanket. The night would be crisp and she suppressed a shiver herself as she squatted beside him, watching him for a spell and wishing she could do more.

'Who are you, Wade Rannigan?' she whispered. 'Are you some hero in a book, or something else? Why do you want to die? And why do I so desperately want you to live?'

An hour dragged by and his chills became worse.

She leaned over him, mopping his brow with a cloth and brushing his matted brown hair away from his forehead. His eyelids fluttered wildly and he muttered Christina's name a half-dozen times, each utterance bringing a clutch to her belly. She told herself she had no right to feel that way and, hell, she didn't know him from Adam, but for some reason she couldn't stop herself.

His teeth began to chatter and he jerked, groaning. He was falling deeper into the fever and the next hours were crucial. If he were going to live this would decide it. But did he have any will left to go on?

Slowly she began to undo the buttons

of her bib-shirt, then pulled the bottom of it from her trousers. It wouldn't do to have him freeze to death after all her work. After removing the shirt, she lifted her chemise, baring herself, and pressed her breasts against his chest as she nestled in close, sharing her body heat. She yanked the blanket over them and clung to him, a thought taking her that of all the men she had lain with in her life, for the first time it felt as if she were filling a need for a loftier purpose.

5

Time passed in a blur for Wade Rannigan. He was vaguely aware of the days flowing by, the warmth of the sun on his face, the chill of the night against his skin. At times he climbed a ladder to near-consciousness, and always any awareness came accompanied by searing pain in his shoulder and snatches of images — the outlaw's mocking face, Christina's beckoning smile and the hazy features of a woman ministering over him — and a bitter taste in his mouth as some sort of liquid was forced down his gullet.

Other things penetrated his stupor, the scent of honeysuckle and the feeling of someone sleeping beside him, though at times he wasn't sure whether these were merely delusions conjured up by his fevered mind. Then he would simply drift back into blackness.

He awoke suddenly, sitting straight up, heart hammering against his ribs. A dull ache throbbed in his shoulder and he drew ragged breaths. Sweat trickled down his face and bare chest.

Morning sunlight glaring and painful, he squinted, struggling to focus. Through blurred vision everything looked like bright splotches but at least the image of the outlaw had vanished, merely a figment of his fevered sleep.

'You stayin' this time?' a voice came from off to his left and he looked up to see a woman standing there, peering at him with something that might have been concern on her face. Memory hazy, he struggled to recollect who she was.

Parker. Charity Parker. She had shot at Latorro and dug the bullet from his shoulder. Saved his life, for whatever that was worth.

'How . . . how long?' His voice was raspy, throat parched. A sling made from his shirt held his arm to his chest.

'Been near to two weeks, Rannigan.

Didn't think you were gonna make it for a spell. You're lucky.' She took a few steps closer and picked up the coffee pot, pouring a cup of brownish liquid.

'Am I?' A note of bitterness hung in his voice.

She passed him the cup and shrugged. 'Reckon some things are worse than dyin', if you put it that way. But why are you in such an all-fired hurry?'

He took a sip of the liquid and the memory of its bitter flavor came back to him and he spat it out. 'Christamighty, you got a notion to finish me off now that I'm better?'

She let out a small laugh. 'Sassafras tea. Helps calm a fever. But you ain't answered my question.'

He glanced away, peering at the ground, a heavy sense of depression taking hold. She had saved him but for what? More empty nights? Hadn't she just prolonged the inevitable?

'You should have let me die . . . ' His voice came barely audible.

You cannot die ... She needs you ...

Christina's words rose in his mind and he tried to pass them off as merely a product of his fever-induced visions, but somehow couldn't quite accept that explanation. He had seen her, hadn't he? No, it wasn't possible. It had to be delirium, though it had seemed so real.

'You're welcome.' Charity's lips drew into a tight line, eyes narrowing. She peered at him for long moments, as if searching his soul. Beneath her scrutiny, he felt a twinge of guilt and more than a little annoyed with himself. He had shown her no gratitude for saving his life, but damned if he could bring himself to thank her for prolonging his wretched existence.

You wanted to live ...

Hell I did ...

With a surge of temper, he tossed the tea into the sand. 'Tastes like horse piss.'

She made a tsking sound. 'Ain't that just like a fella ... '

'How you mean?'

'They take a gal's help when they're too lowly to do anything for themselves then suddenly reckon it ain't good enough when they get better. They get plumb fired-up denyin' they ever needed it in the first place, too. I swear, the West is just plumb full of ungrateful sonsofbitches.'

Bitterness played in her eyes and he wondered why. 'What kind of fellas you been around?'

A shadow darkened her face and her eyes went cold. As she turned away and looked out over the stream, he wondered what the hell he had said wrong.

'I can't figure you, Rannigan,' she said after a few moments of uncomfortable silence. 'You got some kind of death-wish, seems like, but the chances of you pullin' through were about the same as Latorro givin' up bank robbin'. Yet you did and it weren't because of what I was doin', least not totally.' She turned back to him, gaze locking with his. 'You got some will to live, whether you want to admit it or not. You best just accept that and stop actin' like a child who needs pityin'.'

The urge to tell her to go straight to hell was nearly overwhelming but he suppressed it.

Is she right, Rannigan? Is there something inside you clinging to this pitiful existence?

He wanted to deny it, but despite the odds he had survived an ordeal that would have killed most men. Hell, he'd made mistake after mistake lately, courted death with reckless abandon, yet in each case he'd struggled furiously to hold on to life, reverse the odds and step back from the brink of oblivion. Why?

Hell, you got any dreams left, Rannigan? Any hopes?

He wished to hell he knew.

'Who are you?' His gaze focused back on Charity and his tone came low and edged with a certain measure of resentment at her for prying into his soul. 'Who are you really?'

She flinched, but quickly hid the reaction and it puzzled him. For the first time since awakening he really looked at her and standing in the morning sunlight she was a vision. A honey glow glossed her chestnut hair and warmed her skin tones, sparkled from her eyes. She did her damnedest to hide the fact, dressing in men's clothing and affecting the surly façade of a cowhand, but her beauty still came through. Eyes narrowing, he noticed something else: her dark eyes concealed some turmoil or pain, something she struggled to keep hidden.

'Reckon I done told you, Rannigan.'

He shook his head, frowned. 'Don't mean your name. Why are you after Latorro? What's he to you?'

Face cinching into angry lines, she turned away again. But he had glimpsed the look of unadulterated fury. She hated Latorro as much as any human being could hate another; that he was sure of. Her body shook with rage and she locked her arms about herself, as if struggling to rein in her emotions. Moments dragged by and when she at last faced him he saw barely held-back tears filling her eyes.

'If you must know, he's the loathsome sonofabitch who murdered my brother. I aim to see he pays for it.'

He nodded, hanging his head, looking back up. 'So you aim to just stroll right on up to him and fill him full of lead?'

'That's the notion.' Her sarcasm didn't conceal the pain behind her words and he rightly couldn't fault her.

'You'll just get yourself killed. He's a tough *hombre*.'

Indignation flashed across her features. 'What the hell you call what almost happened to you? I wouldn't have come along you'da bled yourself plumb to the Happy Hunting Ground.'

He almost spat out a counter barb, but decided Charity Parker wouldn't take kindly to it and he didn't see a hell of a lot of wisdom in getting her riled up any more than she was already.

'How'd it happen, your brother, I mean?' His voice took on a measure of sympathy. He was all too familiar with losing a loved one, the way it ate away at a man's soul.

Her features softened a notch, grief flooding her mahogany eyes. 'He went into town to make a deposit at the bank. Latorro decided to make a withdrawal at the same time. My brother, he . . . ' Her voice wavered as she appeared to struggle desperately to hold on to her composure. 'He wasn't the type to just let things pass. I ain't sayin' he was the most righteous man to come down the trail, but he had his sense of right and I reckon Latorro wasn't it. He tried to stop the robbery and got himself shot to hell for his trouble. Latorro got away. I swore I'd find him. Wasn't no woman workin' with him then, though.'

'Where'd she come from? Who is she?' He wondered what had made Latorro decide to take on a partner. A woman partner. The queen.

'Damned if I know. She just showed up far as I can tell. Took me six months to track him down and I didn't rightly expect him to have company. Didn't expect him to be caught by no manhunter, neither.'

Wade nodded. 'I was sent after him by the father of a woman he kidnapped. He wants his daughter back, though I ain't so sure Latorro hasn't killed her by now. I caught up to him just as he was robbing the bank in Darkwood. I was takin' him back to Alejandro de la Gato. It's his daughter, Camilla, who went missin'.'

'You planned on hanging him after you got there?'

'Reckon. That's about the best way to make sure he don't hurt no one else. He's dangerous as hell.'

'I can handle him. Would have punched his ticket if you hadn't gotten in the way.'

He heard a taunt in her words but she didn't put much heart in it. He saw ghosts of memories haunting her eyes.

'Your brother your only kin?'

She nodded. 'My pa was killed in an Indian raid and they took my mother. Never did know what happened to her. My brother, he was five years older than me, hid me in a root cellar when it happened, kept his hand over my mouth so I couldn't scream. Those Injuns would have got us if not for that. He raised me best he could but it wasn't easy for us and I reckon I disappointed him in a lot of ways. He worked for some local ranches and I . . . ' Her words died in her throat, as if she'd caught herself about to share a side of herself she seldom let show.

'You what?'

'I got by, Rannigan. That's all you need to know.' Her tone was icy, final, and he knew that was all he'd get from her, at least for the time being.

'Didn't mean to pry, ma'am.' A moment of uncomfortable silence passed between them. 'Figure Latorro's got a big headstart on us. His trail's likely cold by now.'

'He rode southerly.' She ducked her chin towards the trail. 'Reckon it won't take long 'fore we hear word of him.'

He nodded. El Bandolero wasn't one to keep his activities a secret. 'We best start headin' that way, then.' He made a move to push himself up but pain lanced his shoulder and chest and he settled back on to the blanket, sweat springing out on his forehead. Gritting his teeth, he made a second attempt to gain his feet, succeeding. His head spun and his legs wobbled like a new-born calf's and he damn near went down again.

'You ain't in no condition to ride yet, Rannigan.'

'Already lost two weeks. Don't plan to lose any more. That gal's life might depend on it.'

Charity shook her head. 'You best concentrate on gettin' your strength back. After this much time I don't reckon another day or two will make much difference.'

He was forced to agree; he was too

weak to ride and he knew it. He could barely stand.

'Reckon I'd better fetch me another shirt and horse when we reach the first town.'

She nodded. 'Best fetch us some supplies, too. Didn't expect to be holed up for such a spell.'

Wade spent the next few hours moving about the camp and walking along the stream bank. Unsteady at first, he felt the strength in his legs come back after a spell. He found himself easily exhausted, though, and had to rest frequently.

Charity pulled jerky and a can of beans from her saddle-bags and he devoured the meal within moments. With some debate he persuaded her to brew a fresh pot of coffee instead of sassafras tea.

After the meal, Charity wandered down the stream where stands of cottonwoods shaded the bank while he stood staring out at the rippling water. The memory of Christina's vision haunted him, filled him with questions about his desire to join her. While he had to admit something had kept him clinging to this existence, he knew he had never longed for her more than he did right now, and perhaps being with Charity only made that worse. Her company served to remind him life was meant to be shared with another, not lived alone and empty.

He wondered just what made a woman like that so all-fired intent on tracking down and killing a hardcase. Granted Latorro had murdered her brother, but things like that happened in the West far too often. It took a certain breed to live here. Despite that, most folks, especially gals, didn't take up the vengeance trail. That's what manhunters and marshals were for. So why had she?

Was it because she figured she had little else with all her kin gone? Was her life empty in ways he couldn't begin to fathom? He saw pain in her eyes, pain that went beyond the loss of a brother, if he read her right. Whatever the case, he found himself more and more eager to know her reasons.

Sighing, he walked along the edge of the stream. The sun sparkled like diamonds from the water.

A sound caught his attention and he glanced up, halting abruptly and shuffling back out of sight beside a cottonwood. Charity stood in the stream to her waist, scooping water into her hands and letting it pour over her throat as she lifted her chin. Her clothes were draped over a branch. He froze, transfixed by her beauty. Droplets of water sparkled on her skin like jewels and he reckoned she was the loveliest woman he had ever laid eyes on. He couldn't deny the bells it set ringing in his southern temples. Unable to tear his gaze from her nakedness, he shrank back further, praying she didn't catch him watching her.

She finished bathing and stepped from the stream, toweling herself off with a cloth she must have brought from her supplies. As she began pulling on her clothes, she turned and looked straight at him. Heat flushed his cheeks and he quickly averted his gaze.

'Get a good eyeful, Rannigan?' The challenge in her voice came with a playfulness he didn't anticipate. In fact, he expected her to be downright peeled.

'Sorry, was walkin' along the stream and didn't quite expect you to be, ah, well, to be . . . '

She raised an eyebrow. 'Naked?'

He turned away, hoping it wasn't too late to show a measure of chivalry. 'Yeah, that, I reckon. How'd you know I was here?'

She let out an easy laugh. 'Been on the trail long enough to know when I'm bein' watched. Never can tell when some animal's gonna sneak up on a body and figure on makin' you its supper, right, Rannigan?' She tugged her chemise over her head then put on her bib shirt. 'You can turn around now. Reckon you've seen all there is to see anyway.'

'You don't appear particularly shy.' He couldn't get the thought of her in the stream out of his mind and swallowed hard.

She smiled and he reckoned he liked it on her. It fit far better than the angry-at-the world turn her lips normally held. 'Shyness ain't likely one of my virtues. Hasn't been for quite a spell, I reckon.'

'What *are* your virtues, if you don't mind my asking?'

'Most folk claim I ain't got any.' Pain came back into her eyes and he stood there feeling awkward and unsure of himself for one of the few times in his life.

'Reckon they'd be wrong . . . ' was all he could think to say.

'We best get back to camp 'fore you're walkin' bowlegged.' A tease in her voice belied the sadness in her eyes. A flush of heat returned to his cheeks.

She gathered up the cloth and brushed past him, heading upstream.

He followed, hoping she'd kindly forget about the incident, but knowing it wasn't damned likely.

★ ★ ★

Juan Rubio Latorro stared out through the grime-coated shack window, wondering who the gawddamn hell had gotten on his trail. The shack was located outside of Darkwood, whose bank he had hit what seemed like an eternity ago. Mining tools and discarded lanterns littered the small room. Two crates stenciled with the word DYNAMITE sat flush against one wall while a table holding a low-turned lantern rested against another. A hard-backed chair occupied a spot near the door. A roach vanished beneath a pile of canvas bags used for a bed in the far right corner.

Two weeks had passed since he left that manhunter to the buzzards after an unknown shootist damn near blew his head off. He was not a man to forget an infraction, no, indeed, he was not. Rannigan had been working alone, so whoever it was was not likely connected to him.

Another manhunter? Would that foolish old man hire a second bounty man on the heels of the first to make certain events went in his favor? He did not think so. A professional mankiller would have hit him with those shots. No, whoever fired was an amateur, but in the long run that made no difference. All men died the same.

Dark eyes narrowing to a squint, he scanned the outside of the abandoned mining-shack, gaze shifting from the boarded-up entrance of the silver-mine to the shadows reaching from trees under the urging of a bloated moon. He saw nothing suspicious, in fact hadn't for two weeks, prompting him to wonder if the lowly *bastardo* had given up the chase. He did not think it likely. Any man who had hunted him down and shot at him in such a manner would not so soon abandon his quest.

A notion struck him. What if whoever it was had stopped to help Rannigan? While he thought it unlikely the manhunter could have survived, he had seen stranger things happen. *Madre del Diablo*, he had once filled a man full of lead only to have the *bastardo* keep walking about like a headless chicken after he was already dead.

Rannigan wanted to die; Juan had seen it in his eyes. And once a man lost the will to go on nothing could hold him to this earth. Did the mankiller have a spark of life remaining?

'Is he alive?' Juan muttered, lips barely moving. Would that not be something? He had wished for a better game from that *hombre*.

'C'mon, sugar, stop lookin' out that window and show a gal some attention.'

He glanced back at the black-haired woman propped up on her elbows on the canvas bed. She peered at him with a lascivious glint in her eyes. She was nothing more than a spoiled *puta* with a mouth as sharp as a cactus but he had taken a fancy to her generous flesh.

'You should shut your mouth, *mi niña*, before I decide you'd look better in black and blue, eh?'

She glared at him, the pout on her lips tightening to an indignant scowl. 'Oh, Christ ridin' a horse, Juan! I didn't expect to be runnin' from every shadow and sleepin' in varmint-infested old shacks for the rest of my days. A gal needs some creature comforts, don't she?'

He let out a mocking laugh. 'What the hell did you think, *mi niña*? You expected perhaps a fine hotel and servants to attend to your every need?'

Her brow furrowed and the scowl went back to a pout. 'Least you could do is pay attention to me. Even he did that.'

'Apparently not enough for you, no? You should have let me kill the old *bastardo*. It is because of him that manhunter put me through hell for two days.'

'Hell, he is my pa, Juan. And he did

provide right fine for me, way you should.'

'He told that *hombre* I took you against your will and that he paid a ransom. I had half a mind to tell Rannigan the truth, though I gawd-damn thought a man such as he was smart enough to figure it out on his own.'

'He's dead anyway, sugar. Don't make no nevermind now.'

An eyebrow arched. 'Is he?'

'Course he is. I shot him. Was fun, too.' She giggled and he wondered a moment who was the worse of the two. Camilla de la Gato, despite being a fine woman in all the places it mattered, was as spoiled and downright mean as they came. The old fool had provided her with everything she ever desired, the finest schooling, horses, and every luxury a rich man could shove down her throat to replace whatever else it was a real father was supposed to do. Juan rightly didn't know because he had never had one, but he felt certain

Alejandro de la Gato was not it. Camilla had ignored all the teachings of society, or more to the point, spat on them. When he'd hired on as a 'hand to scout the de la Gato compound, figuring it would be easy pickings, she had soon shown him the riches of the de la Gato empire did not lie within a safe. It did not take the old man long, however, to catch wind of Juan's plans and that still puzzled him. He suspected Camilla had much to do with that. She took some kind of peculiar satisfaction out of playing him against her *padre* and Juan had been all for putting a bullet into the old man's brain after de la Gato threatened to blow his *cojones* all the way to Mexico. He should not have allowed her to convince him otherwise, but when Camilla de la Gato wanted something it was hard to deny her.

'I would not be so certain, *señorita*. If your father hired one gringo he might have hired another. Someone shot at us, no? And that someone would have been here by now unless he'd stopped to help Señor Rannigan.'

A sarcastic look turned her face. 'Then why ain't you bein' more careful about your trail? You look like you want him to follow you.'

A thin smile played on his lips. 'Oh, but I do want him to follow, *mi niña*. I do not like looking over my shoulder. I wish to lure this one into the open, checkmate him, eh?'

She gained her feet, folding her arms. He detested the petulant look in her eyes. She was gearing up for another one of her tantrums.

'Everything's just some goddamn game with you, ain't it, Juan? I figure even I am. Just some piece you can move around while it suits your fancy. Well, let me tell you, you goddamn chili-eater, you best start payin' me more mind and providin' the way a fella should for his woman 'fore I decide to go back to my pa and tell him you did force me to go with you!' Spite sparked in her eyes and he felt his blood boil.

He turned fully towards her, taking threatening steps and cutting the distance till she was just within reach.

'I told you to shut your mouth, Camilla. You are nothing more than a lowsome *puta* and you are gawd-damned lucky I do not send you back to him tied across a saddle.'

She spat in his face and a laugh came from her thin lips. Hate glittered in her eyes. Spittle dribbled down his cheek.

Without warning, he backhanded her, the blow connecting with a resounding *clack*! A bleat of pain burst from her lips. She stumbled back against the wall, but didn't go down. Blood snaked from her lips. She glared like a rattler poised to strike.

He stepped towards her. 'Do not ever talk to me that way again, *señorita* . . . I will not be so merciful next time.' His voice came low and menacing and she remained silent for long moments. A malicious light coming into her eyes, she began to laugh, a half-insane giggle that crescendoed to a shrill pitch.

'You know right well how to treat a lady, don't you, sugar?' Her voice came glazed with a practiced coyness that ignited a flame of lust within him and he pressed her hard against the wall, jamming his lips to hers. She kissed him back deeply and he tasted the gunmetal flavor of her blood on his tongue.

He pulled away and she bit at his lip, drawing blood, a wanton look sizzling in her dark eyes.

'We will hit the bank in Porter, tomorrow,' he said and she giggled.

She licked at the blood on his lips. 'Anything for you, Juan, anything for you.'

His dark eyes narrowed. 'You are coming in with me this time.'

Her head snapped back and all coyness vanished from her face. 'What the hell you mean, 'comin' in'?'

'You should have killed the sheriff and watched my back last time. You were nowhere to be seen when I got caught.'

'Goddamn, I hadn't never killed a

fella before, Juan, and it was lucky for you I wasn't there. I got you away from him, didn't I?'

A sly glint shown in his dark eyes. 'You did not seem to have much trouble putting a bullet in Rannigan, eh, *señorita*?'

'Well, he was holdin' you and I couldn't see no other way. 'Sides it was at a distance, like shootin' at bottles. Ain't the same when you gotta look in their eyes.'

'I fail to understand you sometimes, *señorita*. You are two different women, no? One part of you belongs to the old man's world, the other part belongs to Hell.'

'That's the mystery of me, sugar. Fella like you needs some spice in his life.'

'You will come in with me, *mi niña*. I will not argue it with you.'

'Hell, how would it look if someone recognized me? The de la Gato name ain't exactly unknown in these parts.' Her words had something else behind them; he saw it plain in her eyes.

'Keeping your options open, Camilla?'

Her face darkened and her eyes narrowed and he knew he had read it right. Camilla de la Gato was a woman who tired of possessions and people in short order and it would not be long before she grew bored with the life of a bandit. She was leaving an open door back to her father and would soon convince him she had been taken against her will. He had no doubt it would be an easy matter for her to sway him. She could likely talk a donkey out of his tail.

'I hate you, you sonofabitch!' The words came with all the spite she could muster, but even that was a lie.

'The hell you do, *señorita*. The hell you do.' He whirled her around and hurled her to the canvas pile. She let out a strangled bleat as he fell atop her and hoisted her skirt.

6

The sun glazed the wide rutted main street of Porter with topaz but Juan Rubio Latorro pledged it would soon turn to ruby.

At the edge of town, he slowed his horse, the mount he had liberated from Rannigan. A fine animal indeed, it was well trained and a pleasure to ride; Camilla could take lessons from it, at least the first half. He glanced sideways at the raven-haired woman, whose face was locked in a sullen mask. Only a glint of hardness in her dark eyes betrayed the fact she was seething inside. She had complained as bitterly as she was capable of for the better part of the ride to Porter. By the time she finally clamped her mouth shut Juan's blood burned like bad tequila. He might have left her voluptuous carcass for the buzzards to feast on had she not been so skilled at pleasuring a man.

Reining up, he rifled through his saddle-bag, caressing the stick of dynamite he'd brought from the shack. Again the game would change and Juan Rubio Latorro would do the unexpected. He would strike swiftly and the legend of El Bandolero would soon eclipse all others.

Gaze lifting to the street, he watched early risers scurry like rodents along the boardwalks, intent on their petty day-to-day routines. Dark eyes narrowing, his attention settled on a marshal stepping from a café, a soda-sinker in one hand, a newspaper in the other. The lawman began walking down the boardwalk.

Juan looked over at Camilla, who had come up beside him. He ducked his chin at the marshal. 'Do not disappoint me this time, *señorita*. There are many other *putas* in the West, no?'

She cast him a spiteful glare but slipped the Winchester from its saddle boot. 'You sonofabitch . . . ' she muttered.

He gigged his horse into a slow walk towards the bank, Camilla following suit. Hand sliding into his duster pocket, he fingered the black game-pieces in their leather pouch, finding a pawn. Bringing it out, he clenched it within a fist.

Drawing within fifty yards of the bank, he gave the raven-haired woman a slight nod. She reined to halt, lifting the Winchester and sighting down its barrel.

The marshal was walking towards them on the opposite side of the street. Too late the lawman caught a glint of sunlight on metal and glanced up. A startled expression jumped on to his face just as she feathered the trigger. The shot thundered through the peace-ful street. The marshal staggered backwards and slammed into the wall of a building, a starburst of crimson exploding across his boiled shirt. His mouth dropped open and he pitched forward, falling face first to the boardwalk. His sinker rolled across the dusty boards and the newspaper fluttered into the street.

A scream ripped out from a woman twirling a parasol. Dropping the parasol and pressing both hands to her cheeks, her gaze fixed to the fallen lawdog and Juan knew instinctively she was the gringo's wife. A pity. Why should they not be together?

He drew the Colt he had taken from Rannigan and squeezed the trigger.

The woman stopped in mid-scream and scarlet exploded across the front of her canary-colored dress. Shock on her features, she stumbled crazily about and toppled over a rail into a trough, sending a great splash of water across the dust. She lay face down, a hand dangling over the edge, water dripping from her limp fingers.

Other screams rang out, shouts. Townsfolk scurried into shops.

He holstered the Colt, pulled the stick of dynamite from his saddle-bag, then fished a lucifer from his duster pocket. He snapped it to light on a jagged tooth and ignited the wick. With a laugh he hurled the stick at the bank window.

It exploded just as it hit the glass. A roar filled the street and windows shattered, shards of glass spiraling into the air. An awning on the building next to the bank groaned and collapsed, crashing to the boardwalk in a billowing cloud of dust. The bank door had blown open. The manager stumbled out, blood dribbling down his face from lacerations where the blast-driven glass had punctured his flesh.

Juan slid the Colt from the holster a second time and calmly picked him off. He tossed the pawn still in his left hand to the boardwalk; it rolled to a stop beside the manager's body.

He dismounted and tied his horse to the hitch rail. He grabbed an empty saddle-bag, stepped over the manager's body and headed into the bank.

Inside, a cloud of dust shimmered

with rays of diffused sunlight. Glass and splintered wood lay about the floor. A woman lay sprawled near the window, not enough of her left to identify. He heard Camilla gasp beside him.

He made his way to the teller-cage behind which a small man in a visor cap stood frozen with a terrified look on his face.

'You will fill this bag for me, eh, señor?' Juan shoved the saddle-bag at him through the opening.

The man didn't move, trembling visibly.

Juan gestured with the Colt. 'Do not make me ask again, señor.'

The teller nodded, snatched up the bag and began stuffing it full of greenbacks and gold pieces.

The process took only a few moments, then the teller handed Juan the saddle-bag as if he had been told to pat a scorpion.

'Many thanks, señor . . . ' Juan lifted the Colt and put a bullet straight into the man's forehead.

He whirled, grabbed Camilla by the arm and hauled her towards the door.

Juan Rubio Latorro was pleased. He had hit fast and hit hard and this time no manhunter was going to interfere with his escape. At the same time no one would doubt that the infamous El Bandolero had darkened Porter with his presence.

* * *

As false dawn painted the sky with gray, the camp-fire flickered to embers. Wade sat up, pulling the blanket about his shoulders and rubbing sleep from his eyes. Today he felt he would be strong enough to ride, to resume his duties tracking down Juan Rubio Latorro. He should have felt more eager to get on with his mission, but he was forced to admit he no longer felt as focused on the prospect.

He had been alone for too many years and these last couple of days with Charity Parker had started to mean more to him than he reckoned they should. Hell, she was as ornery and sharp-tongued a gal as he'd ever encountered, yet something about her, some hinted-at softness beneath her tough exterior, attracted him, made him want to know more about her life and who she was.

He shrugged off the blanket, the brisk air against his bare chest raising gooseflesh. He glanced at her sleeping form, and in slumber her beauty was more evident. Defenses lowered, the softness came out on her face. His mind suddenly filled with images of her bathing in the stream and a mounting desire to touch her face, feel her in his arms took him.

'I'm sorry, Christina ... ' he whispered, surprised by a sudden welling of guilt. It wasn't as if he had not been attracted to other women since her death; he had been with more whores than he cared to admit. But what he felt growing for Charity Parker somehow wasn't the same. It went beyond simple lust and his useless attempts to fill empty nights.

She needs you . . .

Christina would have wanted him to go on, not live a life trapped in bitterness and some perverted desire to let a bullet release him from his pain. Still, he couldn't suppress the notion he was betraying Christina's memory.

There's a lot you don't know about that gal, he reminded himself. She hinted at things that made him wonder, things she kept hidden and though it was rightly none of his business he wanted to know. She had been deliberately vague, especially where her livelihood was concerned. And when it came down to it Charity Parker was hell-bent on killing a man. Granted Latorro was a sonofabitch and deserved it, but the notion of her ending his life put a strange taste in his mouth.

She missed . . .

Could she have hit Latorro that day? Had she missed on purpose? When all was said and done she certainly could

123

have gone after the outlaw instead of choosing to stay and help a man she had never met. But she had let him go.

Perhaps Latorro wasn't the only conundrum in the West.

With a sigh, Wade gathered twigs and dried leaves and rekindled the fire, then started the coffee brewing. When the coffee was ready he downed a steaming cup then rinsed it out and left it sitting atop the deadfall for Charity when she awoke.

The sky brightened, glowing gold. He gazed toward the trail, wondering where the outlaw had gone. Wade bet it wasn't far. He doubted much time would pass before they got word of his activities. Latorro's previous robbery had ended in disaster; the bandit appeared in need of cash and would likely focus his sights on another target.

They would proceed south. A small town called Porter lay in that direction, with Darkwood a half day's ride beyond. Even if the bandit hadn't headed for the town, Wade needed a new shirt and horse, as well as rations and a gun. He was obligated to keep Gato apprised of his progress, but because Porter had no telegraph office he would have to wait until they reached Darkwood to send a message. He reckoned he had damn little to report where the man's daughter was concerned.

Or did he?

Who was the gal working with Latorro?

You are a fool, señor. You refuse to see what is right before your eyes . . .

Christamighty, he hoped what he was thinking wasn't true.

The sun rose a notch higher. Glassy thin shells of ice melted from the stream-side. Something glimmered in the sand and he reached down, picking up a white chess-piece and turning it over in his hand. The white queen. He stared at it for long moments, wondering what it boded for the task ahead, then tucked it into his trousers' pocket.

'Who's Christina?' a voice came from behind him, pulling him from his thoughts. He turned to see Charity standing there gazing at him, sleep still in her eyes.

'Reckon I don't know what you mean . . . ' He couldn't quite keep the lie out of his voice and had little notion why he didn't tell her straight in the first place.

'I heard you call her name in your sleep a few times. Reckon it ain't rightly none of my business, though.'

He turned to the stream and gazed into the past, a pained look in his eyes. 'No, it's all right. Reckon it's just a mite hard for me to talk about is all. We were to be married . . . '

'Why weren't you?' Her voice softened and he thought he detected a hint of relief, but couldn't be certain.

'She was . . . killed.'

'Powerful sorry to hear that, Rannigan.' Her voice lowered. 'I know how it feels.'

He turned and peered at her, seeing

sympathy in her eyes. She did know; that was plain. But what was more, she cared.

'I reckon you do. And it ain't a feelin' I'd wish on anyone.'

'How'd it happen, you don't mind my askin'?'

His gaze focused on the ground, came back up. 'She was gettin' fitted for a wedding-gown. When she came out of the dressmaker's shop she walked straight into an argument 'tween two gamblers in the street. One of them pulled a gun and shot at the other. He missed.' His voice broke and emotion tightened his throat. 'The bullet hit her. I was comin' out of the bank but I couldn't stop it. It happened too fast. She died in my arms.'

'Tarnation, Rannigan, that's a hell of a thing.'

He nodded. 'Marshal hanged the man who did it, but it didn't make much difference. It didn't bring her back and I've lived with the nightmare ever since.'

'That why you became a man-hunter?'

He shook his head. 'No. Was before that, except then it was just a job and I had planned to give it up before we married. After she died, well, I didn't rightly see no reason to stop and it meant leaving that town behind. I couldn't stay there with all those memories.'

'So you ran from them?'

A measure of irritation took him. 'Ain't what I'd call it. I didn't have the option of hunting down her killer and ending it. It was an accident and I felt cheated.'

Hurt flickered across her face but she quickly hid it. 'I don't blame you for wanting to run from that, Rannigan. I wanted to run plenty of times from things in my past, but they just follow. That was all I meant. No need to get your lather up about it.'

He scolded himself for taking a cheap shot. 'I apologize, ma'am. Just hurts like hell is all. Reckon it always will.'

Her dark eyes narrowed. 'That why you keep tryin' to get yourself killed?'

'Who says I do?' He shifted feet, suddenly uncomfortable.

'You asked me to let you die. Ain't many a man so eager to meet his Maker 'less they figure they ain't got a reason to go on. You didn't have to ask, though. I see it in your eyes, Rannigan. They're empty.' She peered closer at him, an unreadable look crossing her features. 'Leastwise they were.'

'Were?' A knot of emotion cinched in his belly.

She cocked her head, scrutinizing him. 'Somethin's different. Can't quite figure what. But I got a hope.'

'What might that be?'

Crimson mixed with the gold on her cheeks. He reckoned Charity Parker wasn't a gal who blushed often.

'We best be headin' out. We gotta job to do.' Her voice went hard, but her gaze held his and for a moment he saw barely concealed longing within her eyes. Time seemed to stand still and the urge to hold her, kiss her became nearly overwhelming. She suddenly stepped towards him, arms sliding around his waist. He drew her close, the feel of her body against his own as comforting as anything he'd ever felt. The honeysuckle fragrance of her hair filled his nostrils and the familiarity of it all struck him. He hadn't been imagining through a fever. He had smelled her scent before, felt her beside him.

She jerked back, as if caught committing some sin punishable by hell-fire and strode towards her horse. She muttered a curse that would have turned a church lady's hair white and he reckoned she felt nearly as embarrassed as he had when she'd caught him peering at her nakedness in the stream.

He sighed and went to the fire, kicked sand over it. He gathered up the coffee-pot and dumped the remaining brew to the ground. Within a matter of moments they were packed and ready to ride.

She stepped into the saddle, never

once looking at him, and simply said, 'You comin'?'

He nodded and settled in behind her, arm going around her belly. She gigged the horse into motion and they rode at an easy pace in a southerly direction. He couldn't deny the feeling of her body pressed to his gave him notions a decent man wouldn't admit.

The sun climbed higher and the day warmed, air heavy with the musky tang of autumn.

'Any sign of anything?' He knew it was a foolish question but he needed to get his mind off her gently swaying form rubbing against him and the sweet flowery scent of her hair drifting from beneath her Stetson.

'Trail's over two weeks old, Rannigan. Ain't galldamned likely.'

'Porter's another day's ride . . . ' He couldn't recall ever being at such a loss for words in his life.

'No kiddin' . . . ' Her tone was sarcastic and strained and he knew she was still thinking about what had happened at camp and was not in the least comfortable with it.

The day waned and they made camp in a small clearing. When he dismounted his legs shook and his shoulder throbbed, but he felt stronger than expected.

He gathered dried leaves, small branches and twigs and coaxed a fire to life as dusk began to settle. Staring into the flames he grew lost, attention focusing on Latorro. Was the bandit waiting for them in Porter? Would they meet death there? Had Charity in nursing him back to health merely prolonged the inevitable? Why did he care?

He dug the chess-piece from his pocket, gazing at it.

I still got the queen . . .

The hardcase's words echoed in his thoughts and he uttered a humorless laugh. 'Maybe we both do, Latorro . . . ' he whispered, Charity's face rising in his mind. 'And I reckon I'd be dead if not for her . . . '

'You plan on makin' camp or sittin' there gazin' into the fire all night?'

He looked over to see her standing at the edge of camp, a cloth in her hands. He shoved the white queen back into his pocket and gave her an annoyed glare.

''Less of course you wanna watch me take a bath again . . . ' She laughed and walked off towards the stream. His cheeks flushed with heat. Damn that woman, he thought, but the image of her in the water was back in his mind in a powerful way.

They hit the trail with first light. He judged they would reach Porter within an hour or two and wondered what they'd find. A strange premonition of dread overtook him and with it came a thought: Latorro played every game to win, but when you got down to it the bandit had left his last match unfinished. While the outlaw likely thought Wade dead, he damn well knew someone else had shot at him. A man like El Bandolero wasn't the type to let that challenge go unanswered. So why hadn't he returned to make sure Charity wasn't following him?

Because he was waiting for her to come to him. The hardcase was setting another gambit and Wade had little doubt that fact would be borne out soon, perhaps in Porter. Latorro had no notion who was after him, only that someone was, and he would not stray far from the area until the match was concluded.

Rannigan almost smiled, pleased with himself for seeing what was right in front of him this time. While it represented a certain risk to Charity it also presented an opportunity to trap the outlaw as well. And this time he'd be a hell of a lot more careful.

Perhaps he had little wish to die so soon after all.

The premonition of dread became reality the moment they reached Porter.

Townsfolk were scrambling along the boardwalks and women were wailing. Glass and debris littered the planks.

Belly plunging, Wade spotted a body outside the bank. Another form lay on the boardwalk opposite, a marshal's, and two men were hoisting a dead woman from a trough.

'Christamighty, he's been here . . . ' he whispered.

Charity nodded and he felt her body tense. 'Looks the hell like. Weren't long ago, neither.'

They drew up before the bank and dismounted. Charity stopped a woman who had a handkerchief pressed to her face and tears streaming down her cheeks.

'What the hell happened, ma'am?' Wade could tell Charity struggled to make her voice comforting, but was only partially successful. The scene had shaken her up, likely reminding her of when her brother was killed.

The woman looked at Charity through tear-filled eyes. 'They killed my husband . . . He . . . he worked in the bank . . . '

'Who killed him, ma'am?' Rannigan

kept his tone steady.

'A man and a woman. They rode in and killed the marshal and his wife in cold blood then threw dynamite at the bank and shot my poor Wilfred.'

Her words confirmed what he already knew. And told him whoever rode with the outlaw now was aiding him full-time. The thought of it left a sour taste in his mouth and he wagered Alejandro de la Gato wouldn't care much for the flavor, either.

Rannigan's eyes narrowed, gaze lifting to the street. 'Anyone see where they went afterward?'

The woman shook her head and started muttering incoherently. Charity passed her to another woman and eyed Rannigan, a grave look on her face.

'Least we know he didn't go too far.'

'He wouldn't . . . ' Rannigan eyed the end of town, wondering where the outlaw was at the moment.

'You expected this?'

He nodded. 'Or something like it. Latorro told me he never loses but if he just walks away from you he does. You got the better of him that day. Now he's waitin' for you to come to him and finish the game.'

Spite crossed her face. 'Then I'll finish it and that's a puredee fact.'

He gazed at her, saw determination in her eyes, yet at the same time a slight softening of her conviction. Had her resolve weakened a notch? Had she simply needed a reason to let it go? And was he it?

Charity turned, slowly walking down the boardwalk and stopping to stare out towards the end of town. She wrapped her arms about herself, as if struggling for comfort amidst a storm of grief.

His gaze went to the body in front of the bank door and a glimmer of sunlight on ebony caught his eye. Going to it, he knelt and plucked a black pawn from the boardwalk. If he needed confirmation Latorro was luring Charity to her doom that was it. The gambit again.

His fingers curled around the piece, forming a fist.

★   ★   ★

Juan Rubio Latorro smiled and stepped back into the alley. He eased along a wall and out on to a back-street, careful to keep out of sight until he reached the west edge of Porter, where Camilla was waiting.

'Why the hell you grinnin' like a goddamn storybook cat?' she asked, spite in her voice. She sat atop her horse looking down at him. He could tell she was itching to start something but he refused to let her ruin his good mood.

He mounted, peering at her. 'It is because the game has become much more engaging, *mi niña*.'

Her brow crinkled. 'What you talkin' about?'

'Señor Rannigan, he is alive. You did not kill him after all. And he has a woman with him.'

138

'Who is she?' The words came out like a bullet and a flicker of jealously sparked in her eyes. He almost laughed at the ludicrous thought of Camilla showing green.

'If I am not mistaken I would say she's the *señorita* who shot at me. She looks familiar but I cannot place her.'

Her lips tightened. 'I'll just bet she does.'

A laugh escaped his lips. 'Do not worry, *mi puta*. You are the only whore for me.'

She spat. 'You bastard.' Then a smile touched her lips. 'We best not stay so close. That manhunter's got nine lives if he survived that bullet.'

Cockiness settled on his face and he felt a strange sense of elation in his bowels. 'On the contrary, *señorita*. I will leave an easy trail for them to follow. This manhunter, perhaps he has nine lives, but perhaps he also used eight of them with me already, eh?'

'You're gonna get us both killed, you dumb greaser.'

His face darkened. 'I always win. I have told you that. I will not lose to this *bastardo.*'

She leered at him with doubt in her eyes and he laughed, gigging his horse into a gallop. The thought of Rannigan on his trail filled him with giddiness. Camilla's bullet had nearly cheated him of the satisfaction of killing Rannigan himself. Now he would get a second chance. The game was on again. And the winner would take all.

7

Camilla de la Gato pushed through the batwings of the Darkwood Saloon and eyed the barroom. It was typical as far as drinkeries went, though she hadn't rightly been in that many. Her pa, fine upstanding citizen that he was, barely let her set foot outside the ranch unless it was for some function where he needed to be seen as a family man. But he never had been that, had he? He'd stupidly handed over whatever her greedy little heart wanted from day one. While she cottoned to that just fine and dandy it had never provided her with any sense of grounding or a notion she meant anything more than a showpiece to bounce on his knee whenever the charade needed playing. She had dutifully giggled and gleamed and accepted yet another pony or fancy dress for her part in the drama. She had

had the best of everything: clothes, breeding and schooling, but all that still left her lacking in the thing she craved most: excitement. Being so all-fired rich bored a gal plumb out of her skull and when Juan Latorro rode in that day she knew he was her chance to escape her humdrum existence and get her blood racing.

The thought of a bandit living right under their roof had intrigued her, stirred a perverted attraction, and she had decided to play her own little game. Juan wasn't the only one who liked to win, though he was right clumsy about it as far as she was concerned. Juan lacked guile and was too rightly full of himself. She was much more clever and cunning. With her feminine wiles, she could fetch herself almost anything, way she had fetched him. In the final tally she reckoned she'd grow tired of Juan as well, and teach the bastard all winnin' streaks came to an end. She giggled. Juan sure had a kick comin' to his britches. He held his queen, way he put it, but she *was* the queen and he would get her scepter right where he didn't expect it.

A cloud of Durham hung in the air and sunlight arced through the dusty windows, nearly making it glow. She saw men playing poker at green-felt tables but business was light and she wasn't surprised since it was early in the afternoon. Time dusk fell, men would pour in from the local spreads and when that happened she had no desire to be seen in here and recognized — especially in this get-up.

Juan had seen fit to fetch her a saloon gal's corset and blue sateen bodice that heaved her God-given attributes practically to her chin. He got some sort of kick dressin' her up and she reckoned maybe she did, too. Way she'd piled her hair in ringlets atop her head and applied heavy daubs of coral to her cheeks and kohl over her eyes, she figured no one was likely to recognize the daughter of Alejandro de la Gato, but wouldn't push her luck. Christ on a horse, though, the corset was about squeezin' her innards out her throat. She couldn't wait to get out of it, though she reckoned she might make Juan pay for her favors tonight with some of those greenbacks he stole from the bank in Porter. Wouldn't that be excitin'? She'd never actually been a whore before. The thought of it brought gooseflesh to her arms.

Camilla caught sight of the man Juan had sent her to fetch, the barkeep. Juan had told her the fella did him favors back in the early days of El Bandolero and he needed another, now, one that would put an end to that Rannigan fella. She wondered if he weren't plumb loco draggin' things out this way. He was invitin' disaster in her estimation. Him and his dimdot game. Juan should pay more attention to her instead of his silly ruse, but if she didn't help Juan with this he might beat her till she couldn't walk. She liked it rough, but there was a limit and Juan didn't seem to know it.

She threaded her way through the tables and stepped up to the bar. The 'keep was a bony man with a face like a corpse and eyes sunk deep in dark pits. Hell, he was as appealing as a two-headed longhorn but she flashed him a smile dripping with honey.

'Well, well, little lady, what can I do ya for?' His voice came as silky as a canvas nightgown and his gaze locked on her plumped-up cleavage.

'Why, I find myself a mite short on capital at the moment, sir, and was noticin' you might need yourself a lady to help get your customers through the nights. Surely you got a place for little old me.' Her voice was so sugary she wanted to gag but the 'keep lapped it up.

The 'tender grinned and a lascivious light glittered in his eyes. 'Well, I dunno, missy. Reckon I got enough gals. What makes you so special?' He raised an eyebrow, but his line of sight didn't waver from her bosom.

'Oh, I got me talents you ain't even

begun to explore . . . ' She ran her tongue sensually over her candy-red lips. Eating out of her hand, she thought. Men were all stupid.

A brush of cool air at her back made her head swivel and something sank in the pit of her stomach. 'Oh, Christ on a horse,' she whispered, seeing the man who had just come through the batwings. He plucked a Stetson from his head and looked in her direction; she averted her gaze. Last time she had seen that fella she pistol-whipped him from behind and left him trussed up like a Thanksgiving turkey and it was a damned inconvenient time for him to show up.

'What was that?' the 'keep asked.

'Why, I think you ought to just give me a chance, sugar, I said.'

'Didn't sound like — '

'Howdy, Festus,' came a voice beside her and she kept her gaze riveted straight ahead.

'Why, Sheriff, what brings you in here?' The 'keep shifted his gaze from her bosom to the lawdog stepping up to the counter beside her. She felt her heart step up a beat. Christ, she hadn't reckoned on this and likely neither had Juan. If that lawdog recognized her, things could get mighty complicated.

'Just got a message the bank in Porter was hit. Someone used dynamite, blew it half to hell. Murdered the town marshal and his wife, too.'

'Hell and tarnation!' The 'keep slapped the counter. 'Hell of a thing, but what's that got to do with me?'

'Well, jest that from reports it might have been El Bandolero who done it.'

A dark look shadowed the barman's face and worry danced in his eyes. 'Christamighty, Sheriff, I thought you told me — '

'I did. Last I saw of that scalawag I left him in the care of a manhunter named Wade Rannigan. If that *hombre*'s loose again it means Rannigan's dead. Doubt Latorro will head this way, but keep your eyes open all the same.

Can't be too careful with a fella like that.'

'I surely will, Sheriff. He comes in here I'll fill his hide plumb full of scatter-gun spit.'

Camilla let out a nervous giggle. She couldn't help it. Christ on a horse, that 'keep was a brave man with the law standing by, but if he got a look at what was waitin' on him upstairs he'd be singin' a different tune.

'Don't rightly see where that's funny, ma'am.' The sheriff's gaze locked on her. She felt her belly lurch.

'Why, Sheriff, I'd be right foolish to laugh at some other fella's misfortune, wouldn't I?'

'Then what *were* you laughin' at?'

'Only that such a strong handsome man like yourself shouldn't be worried about the likes of some *bandido* coming into town.' She put extra honey in her voice but made sure not to look at him straight on. This man wouldn't be fooled like the 'keep. She could tell his eyes were studying her, searching, and she knew he didn't believe a lick of what she told him.

'I know you from somewhere?' the sheriff asked. 'You look a mite familiar.'

She giggled again, this time intentionally. 'Reckon I'd recollect a fine man like you, Sheriff.'

He shook his head. 'I can't place you now, but it'll come to me. When it does I hope it ain't to your disadvantage.'

Irritation took her and she wished she could just treat him to a measure of her temper, way she did Juan. 'I reckon it could only be to your pleasure, Sheriff.'

The sheriff set his hat atop his head and nodded to the 'keep. 'You see anything you let me know, and miss . . .'

'Yes, Sheriff?' *Christamighty, just get the hell out of here and let me get about my business*, she thought.

'You're still around tonight maybe we'll talk some more in private. I got a notion when it comes to me who you are I ain't gonna like it.'

'Oh, I got a notion you might, honeypie.'

He peered at her another moment, then turned and left the saloon.

She smiled. That little diversion had made her feel as alive as she ever had. Something about fear set her sprites to dancing.

Her gaze returned to the 'keep, whose face had gone a shade whiter. 'Why, sugar, a big brave fella like you ain't afraid of no *bandido*, is he?'

With an air of a bantam cock he shook his head. 'Why, course I'm not a-feared. That fella comes in here I'll fill his lowly hide full of buckshot.'

'How 'bout that job, sugar? A gal's gotta eat. I'd be willin' to let you sample a measure, too . . . '

The grin almost swallowed his face. 'Well, I do have certain quality standards . . . '

'I just bet you do. Why don't you take me upstairs and show me the ropes. I'd be right obliged.' She winked and if it were possible his grin got bigger. He nodded to another dove and she came around the bar. He wiped his hands on a cloth and sidled around the counter. She hooked her elbow through his and they headed for a stairway at the back of the room. On reaching the top, they went down a long hall, the 'keep beaming the entire time. She swore he was a step away from drooling like one of them big ugly dogs that toted a liquor barrel beneath their chins.

He placed his hand on the glass knob as they stopped at a room and she shook her head.

'Huh-uh, not that one. I want the room at the end.' She ducked her chin towards a closed door at the end of the hall and smiled coyly.

He gave her a puzzled look, but nodded. 'Anything for a lady. Reckon you're in fer a treat, missy.'

She giggled. 'That's just what I was thinkin' . . . '

Juan Rubio Latorro stood in the room at the end of the hall, a sly smile oiling his lips. The sight of Camilla gussied up in that bardove's get up brought a certain irony to the game in his mind and he couldn't deny it made his blood race. It was not such a big step from spoiled rich girl to whore and Juan enjoyed the contradiction. But in her case, perhaps they were not so different. Did she not sell herself to him for his favors, for excitement, for the fever that made the blood run fast and hot? He laughed, hard eyes narrowing. It was a fitting role for her, indeed.

Juan lowered himself into a hard-backed chair and ran a hand over his stubbly chin. He had climbed up the outside staircase and through a window, first instructing Camilla he'd be in the last room to the right. The room was sparsely furnished, holding a worn mattress, a small table and the chair he was sitting on.

His mind turned to Rannigan. So the manhunter had lived. He saw it as little short of a miracle, one in the form of that chestnut-haired *señorita* with him. He had seen her before, but where? And why was she after him?

He searched his memory, a hazy recollection coming to him. A small town many miles north of here. Another bank job. He had killed some gringo who thought to make a hero of himself. That was it. As Juan had made his escape he recalled glimpsing a woman, horror on her face as she ran towards the bank. But this woman was a saloon girl, a *puta*. Could they be one and the same?

If so, why would she be after him? Had that gringo meant something to her?

It did not matter. He would teach her the rules of the game. No one got the better of Juan Rubio Latorro. Last gringo who had would find that out as well. And soon. That was the reason he had returned to Darkwood. He planned to pay McKellen back for that little incident three years ago; Juan Rubio

Latorro never forgot — or forgave a debt.

A sound from beyond the door brought him from his thoughts. As the door came open, he pulled the Colt from his holster and drew back the hammer. He centered the aim on the man who came through. Camilla stepped in behind the 'keep and eased the door shut.

'Long time no talk, eh, Señor Blevins?' He stood and the barkeep stopped cold, started to shake like a newborn calf.

'Juan . . . ' His mouth made fish movements.

'I see you did not forget me, Señor Blevins. Me, I never forget my friends, either, eh?'

Camilla giggled. 'Says he would fill you full of shot if'n you came round, Juan. Couldn't keep his peepers off my titties, neither.'

Juan grinned. 'Ah, Señor Blevins, you are a brave man, indeed.'

The man shook harder, as though

about to rattle all his bones loose. 'You-you gonna kill me?'

'Señor Blevins, you misunderstand me. I need a favor from you. That is all.'

'What-what you want?' The 'keep's Adam's apple bobbed.

Juan holstered his gun and moved closer to Blevins, dark eyes locking with the man's dull blue orbs. 'I want someone dead, Señor Blevins. Someone in Porter.'

The man's face twisted with horror. 'I ain't no killer, Juan. You know that. I ran messages for you back when and I was damn glad to do it, yes, sir, damn glad, but I ain't never killed no one.'

Juan let out a derisive laugh. 'It would be well for you to learn, or find someone who can, if you would like to live out the day, *señor*.'

'I'll find someone, Juan. You can count on me.'

Juan grabbed the man's jaw, squeezed, dark eyes probing, condemning. 'See that you do and make sure it is done by tonight. Do I make myself clear, *señor*?'

The man muttered a high-pitched yes and Juan shoved him back. 'W-who's this man?'

'His name is Rannigan. Use a knife. Cut him into little pieces, eh?'

'Christamighty! That manhunter?' Blevins looked as if his heart had just stopped. His face bleached; a tic twitched near his eye.

'He bleeds as any other man. Make sure whoever you get can recognize him.'

The barkeep nodded, glanced to Camilla, who smiled at him like a snake as he backed from the room.

After he'd gone, Camilla glared at Juan and folded her arms.

'What do you wish to complain about now, *señorita*?'

That was all she needed to let loose. 'You're plumb loco! You know that? Ain't goddamned likely he can find someone good enough in this hell-hole to put away Rannigan. You'll just lead that fella back to us.'

'That is what I wish, *señorita*.'

'*What?*' Her voice jumped in pitch and irritation pricked him. 'Are you plumb out of your saddle? He wants to kill you, Juan. Kill you! That gal with him does, too. She already tried it.'

'Señor Rannigan and that *puta* have some surprises coming. It is all part of the game.'

'Let's just leave. He's too close. Forget about him and that gal.'

'No, never . . . ' His voice dropped a notch, turned icy. 'I will finish this game, *mi niña*. As I have said, I do not lose.'

Anger flared in her eyes. 'You sure as hell lost one with McKellen — '

His hand flashed up, knuckles taking her full across the jaw. She stumbled back and slammed into the wall. She slumped to the floor, gazing up at him with a stunned look in her eyes.

'Hell, I have . . . ' He stepped towards her, grabbing her by the hair and hauling her up. He threw her on to the mattress, where she flopped like a rag doll, then began to unbutton his shirt . . .

* * *

Dusk in Porter brought an eerie sense of peace. Few townsfolk were about and the ones who were avoided walking over the crimson blotches soiling the board-walk where the town marshal and bank manager had fallen. The bank door and window had been boarded over, some of the debris swept up and the only merchant with an upswing in business was the funeral man. Folks spoke in hushed voices of El Bandolero, the devil who had ridden into their town in a fury of thunder and blood.

Wade gazed absently through the café window, wishing he could get the sick feeling out of his belly. He was convinced Latorro had used Porter as a maneuver in his perverted game, as much as for monetary gain. The bandit was out there, somewhere, waiting for

Charity to come to him.

The waitress brought their order, beefsteak, biscuits and coffee, then walked away.

He peered at Charity, who stared at her plate.

'Reckon it's been a spell since you ate anything other than jerky and hardtack.'

She nodded. 'Guess you're worth totin' along after all. Didn't have enough money for this since I haven't . . . worked in a spell. You're lucky folks are willin' to give you credit jest on your reputation.'

'If that's your way of sayin' thanks, you're welcome.' He had spent the better part of the day purchasing a new shirt and horse, as well as a Colt at the gunshop. He'd visited the local sawbones, who had looked over his wound. He had forgone the sling, but found mobility in his left shoulder limited and the muscles there stiff as hell.

The remainder of the day he devoted to questioning some of the townsfolk who had witnessed the robbery from behind closed doors. They described Latorro and the woman with him, confirming his suspicions. Latorro had somehow enlisted Camilla de la Gato in his reign of terror. But was the aid forced or given voluntarily?

'You reckon Latorro is headed back to Darkwood?' asked Charity, sipping her coffee.

His brow scrunched. 'Can't see how that'd make sense. He tried the bank there once. Ain't no reason for him to go back.' Even as he said it a gnawing doubt told him he was wrong and that that was exactly where El Bandolero was headed. But why?

'What about that gal with him?'

He shifted in his chair. 'What about her?'

'You been thinkin' something. I can see it in your eyes, 'specially since you got her description.'

He nodded, sighing. 'I figure she's de la Gato's daughter.'

Charity nodded and he felt mildly surprised she didn't show any shock.

'Wouldn't surprise me none.'

'Don't follow.'

'De la Gato's a powerful man. I heard of him. I figure he didn't have much time for his daughter and shoved possessions at her. Maybe she turned out rotten.'

'You got a cynical way of thinkin'. I didn't come to that conclusion so easy and I still ain't sure she ain't been forced somehow.'

'Men ain't the quickest when it comes to women. Latorro didn't force her to do nothin' she didn't want to do. Take my word on it.'

He studied her, judging she was dead serious. 'If that's the case someone's makin' a fool out of me.'

She grinned. 'You reckon that'd be a first?'

'You sure got a way of gettin' under a man's skin.' His tone was only half-serious. Fact was, she got under his skin in more ways than one. He found himself almost wishing he didn't have to chase down Latorro, that he could spend time getting to know her.

She remained silent, gazing out into the deepening shadows of the day. A dark look washed over her face and she suddenly appeared somehow vulnerable, lost, as if the walls she'd put up around her emotions were beginning to crumble.

She looked back to him, mahogany eyes filled with pain, hurt and maybe something else — guilt? Regret? He couldn't be certain.

His voice softened. 'You got somethin' on your mind?'

She looked at her plate, back to him. 'I been thinkin' 'bout what you said, how that gambler bein' hanged didn't bring Christina back.'

His belly cinched and emotion clutched at his heart at the mention of her name. 'Can't say I felt much of anything when he died. Was too filled with emptiness when I realized she'd never be in my life again and all the things we planned to do were never going to happen.'

'When Latorro murdered my brother all I had to live for was huntin' him down and killin' him. I thought about it day and night, tasted it.'

'And now?'

She shrugged. 'Now I wonder if killin' him will help anything. Maybe I should just leave him to the law.'

'Ain't known you long, but that impresses me as a right big change.'

'Wasn't nothing else in my life before . . . ' Her words came lower, almost inaudible.

'And now there is?'

'No,' she said at last. 'Maybe there ain't. But killin' him won't bring my brother back and beyond that I ain't got nothin' anyway.' She uttered a cheerless laugh. 'Hell, worse than nothin'.'

'Can't say you ain't right. Fact is, I got a notion you are. But I know how Latorro's mind works and he ain't likely to see it the way you do. He wants you to follow him. I think that's why he hit the bank in such a big way. He left you a clear calling card that he was ready and waiting.'

'I'm thinkin' of disappointin' him . . . '

Before he could stop himself, he reached across the table and clasped her fingers. She didn't pull away and he reckoned her hand in his felt half-way to heaven. 'I got no choice but to track him down. I have to find out the truth about that man's daughter and he'll discover I'm alive sooner or later and come after me. Way I figure it, you can leave now and let me stop him 'fore he comes after you.'

Their gazes locked. 'No, I go with you and see it through to the end.'

'No need to risk any more than you already have. I'll get him for you, Charity, mark my words.'

A glint of protectiveness sparked in her eyes and she drew her hand away. 'Hell, you will. We'll ride out together at first light.'

He nodded and they finished their meal in silence. Why had she changed her mind so fast? A moment before she appeared ready to quit, told him as much. A notion took him she had been wanting him to give up on Latorro as well. Was that why when he told her he had to finish it she had insisted on coming with him?

He wagered that was the case. If so, it meant she had feelings for him. He couldn't deny that filled him with a rush of warmth he hadn't felt for a very long time.

Leaving the café, they stepped out on to the boardwalk and began walking towards the small hotel at the edge of town. Darkness had settled over the streets.

A chill breeze came with the night; it stirred genies of dust along the boardwalks and whispered through awnings and eaves. Charity remained silent beside him, keeping her gaze focused ahead.

A sound caught his attention, scuffing, furtive, and at first he thought it might be an animal foraging for food in the alley just ahead. Except that with the sound came a shiver of that manhunter's sixth sense that something —

A man stepped from the alley, a look of viciousness on his shadowy features. Wade stopped, arm going out in front of Charity, halting her. The man, an obvious hardcase, took a step forward and something glittered in his hand. A dagger-style knife with a long tapering blade commonly referred to as an Arkansas Toothpick.

'What the hell you want, stranger?' Wade kept his voice steady, though his heart started to pound against his ribs. The hardcase swayed the blade left then right, obviously practiced with it.

'I want your money, *señor*, and maybe your woman, eh?' A grin slid over his coarse dark features. 'Now, *señor!*'

Wade tensed, hand slowly reaching into his pocket and pulling out a few silver dollars. He had little money on him.

'That's it?' The man tried to sound disappointed but his tone betrayed him and told Wade he had other things in mind. The robbery was just a ruse. 'That is not enough, *señor*. It is not enough at all.' Without warning, he lunged. Some instinctive sense of self-preservation made Wade jerk sideways as the attacker thrust the blade. The point sliced through his shirt but missed his flesh. He tried to bring his left up in a short chopping blow, but pain shot through his shoulder and the punch came without much power. It rebounded from the robber's jaw, doing no damage.

The hardcase laughed and drew back for another swipe with the knife. Wade braced himself for the attack.

'Run!' he snapped at Charity.

'Hell I will!' Charity yelled but he had no time to argue the point. The knife whisked towards his belly. He twisted, snapping the heel of his right palm against the man's chin.

The knife swished by Wade's side, missing. The blow clacked the man's teeth together, momentarily stopping him in his tracks.

The attacker recovered before Wade could move on him, and swung a fist. The punch bounced off Wade's temple and stars exploded before his eyes. He staggered back, slammed into the wall, air exploding from his lungs.

The hardcase whirled, started for him again, knife out-thrust.

A heavy thud sounded and the man let out a startled curse, blinked, staggered in his step. Charity had balled her hand into a compact fist and swung at the back of the knife-wielder's skull.

She let out a yell and kicked at the bandit's knife-hand, contacting. The move should have sent the blade sailing but didn't. He managed to hold on to his weapon and take a step towards her.

Wade, recovering, threw himself at the man. He hit the fellow hard, sending him stumbling across the boardwalk into the street. The hardcase, nimble as a cat, kept his feet and whirled just as Wade lunged at him from the board-walk.

The attacker swung the blade wildly, nearly cleaving off a piece of Wade's hide. If he hadn't dived sideways the fight would have ended right there, along with his life. The move threw him off balance and the hardcase moved in for the kill.

Charity leaped from the boardwalk and was suddenly attached to the *bandido*'s back.

The man threw himself right then left, like a bucking bronco, struggling to throw her off as she jammed an arm across his throat and tried to shut off his air. With a roar he heaved her from him. She landed hard in the dust, groaning.

The hardcase spun, arcing the blade around to finish Wade.

Wade's hand seemed to blur as he snapped the Colt from its holster. He triggered a shot, sending lead into the man's brisket and kicking him backwards.

The attacker landed on his back in the street, making gagging sounds as blood bubbled from his lips. The blade flew from his grasp and landed a few feet away.

Charity reached her feet, brushed off her trousers and bib shirt. Wade holstered his gun and went to the fallen man. He knelt, grabbing the man's shirt in his fist and jerking him up.

'Help . . . help me . . . ' The man's words were liquidy. 'Doc . . . '

'Tell me why you came after me. You were after more than money. I'll get you to the doc after that.'

'Man . . . Blevins . . . hired me to kill you. Didn't know about that gal . . . '

'Who's this Blevins? Where is he?'

The man coughed a spray of blood. 'Darkwood . . . '

His head slumped back and his eyelids fluttered closed. The bandit lay still and Wade knew that was all he'd get out of him. But it was enough. He had no idea who Blevins was, but decided only one man could have set up such a move.

He glanced at Charity, face grim.

'Reckon Latorro just sent us word he knows I'm alive.'

She nodded. 'He went back to Darkwood . . . '

'So it seems. Reckon Darkwood's a four-hour ride at a gallop, half a day at a steady pace. We'll set out first thing tomorrow.' He looked back to the dead man. 'Don't reckon anyone will miss this one.'

A sinking feeling inside told him it wouldn't be the last body on the trail to El Bandolero.

8

A sense of destiny gripped Wade Rannigan as he and Charity saddled up and set out along the trail to Darkwood.

The sun peeked above the horizon, splashing the hardpack with blood-colored ribbons of light. A portrait in scarlet, the woodland appeared funereal and forbidding. Melting frost dripped from leaves like liquid rubies. Even the peaceful sounds of morning creatures did little to dispel the feeling.

The feeling that El Bandolero had drenched the West in blood.

The horse, a sorrel, swayed gently beneath him but seemed given to skittish turns. Twice he'd been nearly thrown as a snake slithered across the trail.

He shot a sideways glance at Charity, who rode in stoic silence, gaze riveted to the trail ahead.

Juan Rubio Latorro, El Bandolero, awaited them in Darkwood. Wade had little doubt Latorro aimed to finish the game and he reckoned if there were a prize to be won in any of this it was Charity Parker's life, not the rescue of de la Gato's daughter, who might be little better than the hardcase himself.

Latorro had never lost. Wade Rannigan was a man looking to die. The odds sure as hell didn't appear in Wade's favor.

Are you lookin' for that, Rannigan? Or has that changed?

He sighed, a voice somewhere inside him confirming what he suspected, maybe what had been right in front of him all the time. Camilla de la Gato's involvement in this case hadn't been the only thing he'd missed seeing. He did want to go on and the reason was the woman beside him.

'You think that gal's pa knows she's in with Latorro?' Charity asked, breaking her long silence.

'Ain't sure yet she is in with him.'

She let out a scoffing *pfft*! 'Get your head out of the sand, Rannigan. She's as poison as they come.'

'What makes you such an expert?'

'I know fool's gold when I see it.'

As he glanced over, a dark look crossed her features, a reflection of unknown trials and loss that told him Charity Parker had lived a life far beyond her years. His gaze settled forward again, and he wondered exactly what she had been through to make her the way she was; he reckoned it was more than the loss of her parents at a young age.

'Yeah, I reckon you do,' he answered at last, voice low.

'You ain't answered my question.'

He shrugged. 'Wish I knew. Makes the difference between me bein' played for a fool and havin' to break God-awful news to a father.'

'Maybe he don't know. You said he paid a ransom.'

He nodded, face turning contemplative. 'Old man said he did. Latorro said something funny 'bout that, though. Asked me why he had to rob a bank if he'd been paid all that money. I got a notion he wasn't lyin'.'

'You gonna take the word of an outlaw on that?'

He shook his head. 'No, reckon I ain't. There's a telegraph office in Darkwood. I owe her pa a report and likely all I'll say is I got a lead on her whereabouts.'

She nodded. 'I'll have me a parley with the sheriff while you do that. I figure we'll need all the help we can get.'

He wanted to talk to the sheriff as well. Latorro had some reason for choosing Darkwood or he would have surprised them in Porter, instead of sending an amateur to do his dirty work.

'Best we go together. Latorro's lookin' to get you, too, remember.'

Indignation crossed her face. 'I can

take care of myself, Rannigan. Always have. Maybe always will.'

'I don't like it.'

'You don't have to. You ain't got a choice. Ain't no fella about to tell me what to do. You best get that in your think-box right now. It'll make life a hell of a lot easier on you.' A smug expression turned her lips and he cursed her for being so goddamn difficult and beautiful at the same time. ''Sides, it's broad daylight. He ain't likely to strike right off.'

'Suit yourself,' he conceded. Her mind was set and he saw no use arguing with her.

They rode in silence for long moments. The sun climbed higher and the day warmed.

She eyed him and he saw something behind that look, some thought she'd obviously been chewing on for most of the ride.

'What happens after we get Latorro, Rannigan? I mean, assuming it comes out our way. You go on tryin' to find a bullet with your name on it?'

The question stung more than it should have. 'Reckon maybe not. I been makin' a lot of mistakes lately. Been lucky I ain't got my wish but sooner than not the Devil'll catch up with me. Maybe Latorro will be my last case.' He wondered if his words surprised her as much as they did himself. He wondered if he weren't just as big a conundrum as Latorro.

She peered at him and he got the notion she was deciding whether he was telling the truth.

'Ain't many a gal who could live wondering whether her fella might not come back from day to day, Rannigan. Be a hell of a life.'

'You lookin' to be one of them women?' he asked before he could stop himself.

'Pshaw! Don't you just wish!' Her reply came too fast and he saw a hint of crimson touch her cheeks.

'Why you so tough, Charity?'

Her features tightened. 'Told you

— growin' up without a ma and pa and fendin' for myself with my brother.'

'Reckon I see more to it than that. You ain't tellin' me the whole truth.'

'Don't rightly care what you think.' Something in her tone said she did and he smiled an inward smile of satisfaction at ruffling her feathers.

A sudden sense of menace invaded his mood and his gaze locked on the trail. His hands tightened on the reins and his heart picked up a beat. Something felt wrong, the way it had before Camilla de la Gato shot at him.

'Rannigan . . . ' Charity's voice came low and she didn't look at him.

'Yeah?' His voice was distant, attention riveted ahead. The hairs on the back of his neck stood up in a tingling wave.

Something's wrong, Rannigan. You feel it but can't see it. It's him; he's close . . .

'I ain't quite what you think I am,' she said in a voice so low he barely heard the words.

Something caught his attention in the trail ahead. Sunlight glinted off a small object lying on the hard-pack and he reined up.

Charity halted beside him, a puzzled expression crossing her features.

Gaze shifting left and right, he dismounted and went forward, reaching the object. Scooching, he picked it up, turned it over in his hand then closed his fingers around it and straightened. He went back to his horse and stepped into the saddle.

Charity eycd him. 'What is it?'

He cast her a serious look then tossed her the object. She caught it, frowned. It was a black pawn.

'He's been here and he wants us to know it.' Face grim, Wade's eyes focused ahead. 'I'll say one thing for him, he's an arrogant bastard.'

She tossed the piece to the ground. 'He ain't arrogant, he's plumb loco.'

Wade nodded and gigged his horse into a slow walk. Latorro had been here, wanted them to come forward, but why? Since the man he'd sent to dispose of them had never returned from his mission, the bandit knew they would come to Darkwood. Wasn't a chess piece on the trail a bit of an over-kill?

Or did he have something else in mind?

Just ahead to the left, a light flared.

'Christ,' he whispered, heart leaping into his throat.

'What's wrong . . . ' Charity started.

'Turn around — now!'

'Rannigan, you gone plum loco . . . '

Wade jerked hard on the reins and sent the horse in a whirl. 'Turn around! Get the hell out of here, Charity!'

She complied, reining around and heeling her horse into motion.

They made it less than a hundred feet before the trail behind them erupted with a tremendous roar and a flash of blinding light. An explosion of dirt, twigs and leaves pelted the ground. A hammering blast of air slammed into his back with stunning force.

The horse stopped short, reared, neighing in mortal terror. Wade was vaguely aware of Charity beside him, her mount following suit. She tore loose from the saddle and flew sideways. The horse bolted down the trail, clods spewing from its hoofs.

Wade's sorrel danced left, skipped right, started to buck. Under normal circumstances he might have held on and got it gentled, but pain splintered through his shoulder and made his left arm numb.

The horse shot straight up and kicked out. Wade's teeth clacked together and air burst from his lungs as the animal slammed back on to the hard-pack with a bone-jarring jolt. He canted sideways, boot-toe coming half out of the stirrup.

Wade gripped the reins with all his strength, struggling to hold on. He might have made it if another explosion hadn't ripped through the morning. This one came a hundred yards south of the first. A blast of air slapped him forward and the horse bolted. Foot not secure in the stirrup, Wade jerked sideways then backwards as the sorrel hurtled forward. Wrenched out of the saddle, he felt suspended in mid-air for an instant before falling. He hit the ground hard, rolling instinctively. Agony seared his shoulder and pebbles and twigs bit into his sides. He came to a halt twenty feet on, spitting dirt and cursing.

Shaking his head, he pushed himself to his feet, panting, every corner of his body aching. His gaze rose to Charity, who had gained her feet and was brushing herself off.

'You picked a goddamn good time to forget about your death-wish, I'll give you that much, Rannigan. But I'm gonna be pickin' burrs outta my britches for a week.'

'You should have bought a better mount, *señor*,' a voice snapped out from down the trail. 'Perhaps one such as this, eh?'

Wade and Charity's gaze lifted

simultaneously. A hundred yards down the trail, Juan Rubio Latorro patted the neck of Wade's former mount and grinned. He had the horse angled sideways across the trail, notched to the right. Clouds of dust wafted about his form, giving him an almost ghostly quality.

'I will be waiting for you in Darkwood, *señor*. I am sure you will not disappoint me.' With that the bandit reined around and kicked the horse into a gallop.

Wade's hand slapped for the Colt at his hip. The gun cleared leather and came up in a blur. He jerked the trigger three times. The bullets missed. The distance was too great.

He stared at the retreating outlaw until the hoofbeats faded and a heavy silence fell across the surroundings. Holstering the gun, he looked at Charity, who had a question in her eyes.

'We go back for the mounts?'

He shook his head. ''Bout the same

distance back or forward. It's gonna be a hell of a walk.'

*   *   *

The door of the mining shack burst open and Juan Rubio Latorro stepped inside. He was *mucho* pleased with himself and he had decided to celebrate by letting Camilla pleasure him before he went to pay Blevins another visit and arrange a welcome for the manhunter.

He had played the game well today. Oh, he had not intended to kill Señor Rannigan and that *puta* on the trail, just as he had not intended they truly meet their demise by the hand of that *bandido* last night. No, that would have deprived him of the full victory but he had more faith in Señor Rannigan than that. That was why he was taunting him and his *puta*, maneuvering them around the board, disabling his opponents piece by piece, until their defenses were worn away and winning was assured. It would have been much

184

too easy to simply surprise and kill them so soon — or would it have been? Perhaps not. Despite the wish for death Juan had seen in the gringo's eyes, Wade Rannigan would fight to the finish. A man of many faces, much like himself. The *señor* made mistakes but quickly compensated for them. No, catching him unawares would not be as easy as it appeared. And a quick game held no satisfaction anyway.

'Where the hell you been?' Camilla de la Gato snapped, as he shut the door. She stood across the room, next to a window.

'Miss me?' He grinned and her eyes narrowed to angry slits. If looks could kill his body parts would have been scattered half-way to Texas.

'The hell I did! I'm jest goddamn sick and tired of being cooped up in this goddamn shack waitin' for you to get done playing your loco games.'

She was still seething over the beating he had given her at the saloon. A livid bruise took up half her jaw. A prickle of irritation intruded on his agreeable mood.

'Señor Rannigan and his woman are on their way here, *señorita*. I must make certain they are welcomed.'

Her dark eyes flamed. 'Christ, ain't it bad enough you practically sent them a telegraph tellin' 'em we was here? Goddammit, Juan, just kill them. I'm tired of this place. You promised me more excitement.'

'I do not recall promising you a thing, *mi puta*, and we will stay until the game is finished. I have other debts to collect on as well, eh?'

She folded her arms across her breasts and her lips pursed into disapproving lines. 'That Rannigan ain't no one to fool with and that gal with him sure as hell wants to put a bullet in your sorry hide. I'm tellin' you one of 'em is gonna get you.'

'You may only tease the bull so long, eh?' The mocking came back to his voice and he saw it annoyed her plenty. 'Do not worry yourself, *mi niña*. They will die soon.'

A malicious glint sparked in her eyes. 'If'n you were a real man, you'd provide better for me and we'd go off somewhere together.'

Heat flooded his face and his belly knotted. He did not like it when she ridiculed him in that way. He would let her get away with many things, but not that. Eyes narrowing, he took a threatening step towards her.

She spat. Saliva dribbled down his face and he stood for a moment, looking at the smug expression on her features and the goading glint in her eyes and something inside him turned to ice. His voice lowered. 'That is a damned ugly habit, *mi niña*. I do not like it.'

She giggled. 'Don't say, you dumb chili-eater.' She began laughing harder, her lips getting that churlish air of superiority he detested.

'*Señorita*, you should have shut your mouth . . . ' With explosive suddenness, he hit her with the back of a fist. His knuckles collided with her mouth and sent her stumbling backwards into the wall. She slumped to the floor, head hanging, blood dribbling from her smashed lips.

He let out a roar and lunged after her, grabbing two handfuls of her blouse and hoisting her to her feet. She peered at him with a dazed expression, and he hurled her atop the canvas bed. With great effort, she lifted her head and dragged the back of her hand across her lips, wiping away a snake of blood. She looked up at him, hate behind her eyes.

It was all he could do not to kill her then. It was by supreme will-power alone he did not. 'You would do well to listen closely, *señorita*. The West has many whores. I do not need you. Do not forget that.'

A defeated look replaced the glaring hate, with it an air of fearful respect. She crawled over to him, wrapping her arms around his thigh, and began kissing his trouser-leg.

He jerked his leg free and strode to the door. She stared up at him with a pitiful pleading expression and he let out a laugh. 'I am no longer in the mood, *señorita*. You have ruined it for me. I will find myself a whore at the saloon.'

'I'll make you happy, Juan, you'll see. Please don't get no whore . . . '

'I always win, *mi niña*. It does not matter whether it is against that manhunter or a lowly woman such as you.' He opened the door.

'Where you goin', Juan? Please don't go to the saloon. Don't leave me here by myself again. Please. I'll go loco.'

'You will live. That manhunter and his woman will be here by morning. I must ask our friend Blevins to arrange to have a couple *bandidos* receive them. I am a most thoughtful host, do you not think?'

'I think you're a bastard.'

'I am worse than that, *mi puta*. I am El Bandolero.'

* * *

'*You son of a bitch!*'

The words came out a screech as Camilla de la Gato stared at the closed shack door after Juan Rubio Latorro had gone. Rage made her heart pound and her paining face flush with heat. She crawled atop the canvas bed and into the corner, pressing her back to the wall. Wrapping her arms about herself, she drew deep breaths, fighting to regain her composure and stop shaking.

She hated him.

She hated him for beating her and for leaving her here by herself and for just being everything he was. A bastard pure and simple.

A thought struck her unbidden and she uttered a high-pitched laugh that came dangerously close to insanity. She hated him but craved his approval and attention, in any fashion, and constantly, and when she won them only then would Juan Rubio Latorro become a waste of her time. The excitement would be gone. And so would she. A possession gained was a possession no longer wanted. That would never change. *She* would never change.

She cursed, wondering where the hell her life had taken its first bad turn on the trail. Considering all her father had bestowed upon his only child, she should have turned out better. All the fancy schoolin' had been wasted on her; she'd learned to talk and cuss and spit like a ranch hand just to make him dance through hoops whenever he needed her to show her breeding, but somewhere along the way it had become part of her. Or perhaps it had always been her nature. The art of manipulation came easy and fast and damned if she didn't enjoy it. Something about the power it gave her over folks, especially men, excited her, though she had to admit Juan was different that way and that aroused her all the more. But even the famous El Bandolero would learn a thing or two before she was finished with him.

She clenched her teeth and glared at the closed door. If he thought he had defeated her he had another think coming. She let him see only what she wanted him to see, think what she wanted him to think and she had put on a damn fine performance a few moments ago. Oh, it hadn't been easy, considering how all-fired peeled she was at him for hitting her the way he had, but she could see it in his eyes: he had reached his limit with her and might be inclined to find himself someone else and she couldn't have that. Hell, she reckoned she didn't have a lot of Christian qualities but she demanded loyalty from her fella, least till she got tired of him.

She would be the one who decided when the time was right to move on and no one else, not Juan, not her pa, and not some horseshoe-blessed man-hunter and his gal.

Juan was plumb loco toying with that fella and it was taking too much of his attention, time that belonged to her.

Besides, any men Blevins hired wouldn't get the job done and Juan damn well knew it. But it gave her a notion, one that would get her out of this shack and prove to Juan he needed her and wanted her.

It would also get even with him for treating her that way.

She giggled, pleased with herself. She wondered what Juan would think when he came back and found her gone. He wouldn't expect her to defy him after the cowering performance she'd put on. Likely he'd be right pissed about it. But that wouldn't matter, 'cause in the end he'd see she'd done him a favor.

She'd persuade Blevins to tell her who he'd hired to go after the manhunter and that gal. Then she'd round up the fellas and help them kill Rannigan, grab the woman and bring her back here. She'd make that hussy tell her why she was after Juan and then maybe she'd kill her first person close up. She had to admit the idea had grown on her since seeing that marshal die by her hand; it raised a surge of feverish excitement in her veins.

Another giggle.

She stood, shaky at first, but gaining strength as she grabbed a Winchester from a corner and went for the door. 'We'll jest see who wins this game, *mi amor*,' she said in a spiteful voice and stepped out into the day.

* * *

Dusk brought a brisk chill to the air. Ribbons of shadows wavered under breeze-swayed trees. The first stars glittered in the sky.

Wade and Charity stopped upon reaching a small clearing. Every muscle in his body felt as if it were locking up and his feet likely had blisters. He now knew what Latorro had felt walking all that distance, and knew it was the outlaw's way of getting even.

'We can camp here for the night.' He looked at Charity, who nodded. 'We head out early, we can make

Darkwood in a few hours.'

She frowned. 'Ain't never seen the likes of a man such as that. He's puredee evil.'

'Inclined to agree. I best do the job right and make sure he's swingin' at the end of a rope this time.'

'We best do it right, Rannigan.' She walked towards the edge of the clearing and looked off into the distance. She had been sullen most of the day, untalkative. He found himself wishing he could comfort her, but felt unsure how to approach it. His skills in that direction had suffered as much as his soul since Christina's death. He was used to bargirls, whose only comfort came from payment rendered at the conclusion of a night's ministrations. Charity required more. If she risked revealing herself to him she expected payment in emotion. He hoped somewhere inside him he still had that left to give.

She had been about to tell him something just before the explosion, he recollected. He wondered what it was but she hadn't volunteered the information and he wasn't inclined to press her on it. Charity Parker told things in her own time, no one else's. She wasn't quite what he thought she was, she had said. What did that mean? He'd been with her better than two weeks and knew little more about her than when they'd met. That notion should have made him more cautious but instead it brought a disturbing guilt.

Because he hoped Christina could forgive him for falling in love with Charity Parker.

She needs you . . .

Trying to keep his mind off the notion, he gathered sticks and dried leaves. He pulled a lucifer from his pocket and moments later a fire blazed. With a rumble, his belly reminded him the horses had run off with their supplies and coffee.

Dusk deepened into night and the moon came up bloated and bright. Stars glittered and wispy clouds looked like charcoal cotton against an indigo background.

El Bandolero . . .

Latorro waited for them somewhere in or near Darkwood. It left Wade in an unfamiliar role. He was used to tracking down hardcases, dispensing justice. He was the stalker, not the stalked. In the final tally, Latorro seemed to hold the advantages as well. He knew Wade was coming and would be watching his every move. He was also physically stronger. Wade was wounded, exhausted and hungry. He was still fast with a gun but would that matter?

Was there an evening factor? Perhaps. Wade was no longer the reckless pursuer El Bandolero had first encountered. He had reason to use caution now, take fewer chances: Charity. But so far that hadn't done him much good, had it? Latorro was running circles around him. Yet in a chess match sometimes a player became too involved with his own strategy and lost sight of what his opponent was planning. Could Wade take advantage of that?

Why had Latorro chosen Darkwood? Was that somehow the weakness in his game? The outlaw could have made Porter the battleground but hadn't. No, Latorro had some other reason for holing up near the town. But what?

A sound pulled him from his thoughts and he saw Charity coming up to the camp-fire, an unreadable look on her face.

'Where you been?' he asked, having lost sight of her while he built the fire.

'Just off thinkin', Rannigan. Gal's allowed to do that, ain't she?' Her tone came with a measure of challenge and irritation that surprised him.

'You sit on a cactus or somethin'?'

'Be a hell of a lot sharper than your wit, Rannigan.'

He took the sudden notion he had fallen in love with a rattlesnake.

His gaze dropped and he stared at the ground for a moment, then he looked back to her. 'I been alone a long time, Charity. I ain't used to talkin' to a woman and I ain't used to the things I've been feeling the past few days.' His belly cinched and his heart stepped up a notch. 'After Christina was killed I shut everything off inside. I spent years lookin' for a way to join her, least I thought I was. Now I gotta figure maybe something inside me wanted to go on, wanted a second chance at what her and I never had.'

She stood there staring at him, a pained look in her eyes. 'Please, Rannigan . . . ' Her voice was almost pleading.

She needs you . . .

'I want that chance now, Charity. And somehow I know Christina would want it for me, too. Like I said, I aim to quit after I finish this case, assuming it don't kill me, but I can only do that if . . . ' His voice broke and words lodged in his throat.

'Nooo, please . . . ' Her voice trembled and she turned away.

He went to her, gripping her

shoulders and turning her towards him. A tear wandered down her face.

'You, don't know what you're sayin', Rannigan, you don't know . . . '

'I *do* know, Charity. And it ain't something I expected. I got feelings for you I never thought I would have for any woman again.'

'You can't love me!' The words came out in a scream and she pulled away, breaking his grip and stepping back. More tears came. Her lips quivered. 'You don't know me, Rannigan. You don't know what I've done, what I am. Once you found out you wouldn't want me.'

'Christamighty, I know you got a hard shell around you — '

'I'm a whore, Rannigan! I'm a goddamn saloon whore!' Her body shuddered with sobs and she wrapped her arms about herself. She suddenly looked small and vulnerable, in need of protection and understanding, but for the moment he was unable to give them. The words stung. It was the last thing he expected, though maybe the signs had been there all the time and again he had not seen what was right in front of him. God knew he wasn't the most virtuous of men; he'd been with enough doves in his time, but the notion of what she was turned him inside out.

She'd been with other men. Many of them. Bought and paid for and on to the next. Christ, it made gall burn in his throat but he was a hypocrite if he judged her for that. He reckoned he didn't rightly know how to get past what she had said and didn't know that his death-wish hadn't finally come true, because hearing those words was as close to dying as anything he'd felt since Christina left him.

He stared at the ground, confused, mind wandering, pain gripping his heart. He was conscious of her sobs, the crackle of camp-fire flames and the throbbing ache of his own hurt.

When at last he looked up, she wasn't looking at him, just focused off somewhere distant.

He struggled for words, voice low. 'Hell, I ain't exactly the most righteous man — '

'Don't you understand, Rannigan?' she snapped, gaze locking with his. He reckoned he'd never seen so much pain in anyone's eyes, least when he wasn't looking in a mirror. 'I ain't worthy of you. I have lain with men for money, a lot of men, Rannigan. I ain't proud of it, but it was the only way I could survive. There was nothin' else for me after my ma and pa were gone and by the time I grew up I found out I could use what God gave me to make a livin'. My brother, God bless his soul, did his best, but we just couldn't get by.'

'What'd he think of you doin' . . . what you did?' The words came hard.

'He hated it, oh, he absolutely hated it. But he couldn't stop me, neither. Best he could do was follow me around and try to protect me if a fella got rough or something.'

Wade bowed his head, sighed, looked back to her. 'You asked me what I wanted after we got through with Latorro. You asked me if I would still be lookin' to find that bullet with my name on it. I'm telling you plain you would never have to live a day worrying I wouldn't come home because of that. I'm tellin' you I got every reason to live now. But I'm askin' you the same question: after we get Latorro you plan on going back to bein' a whore?'

She didn't hesitate. 'No, Rannigan. I can't go on with it. Bein' with you these past few weeks has been as close to really livin' as I ever came. I lost my pride and self-respect when I turned sixteen. I reckon maybe now I got a notion where they went. I don't know what I'll do, but I won't go back to bein' a whore.'

He nodded, knowing she meant it. He went to her, taking her into his arms, holding her tightly for long moments. She pulled back and pressed her lips to his, kissing him deeply without reservation. He reckoned it was the closest thing to heaven he'd ever felt. Despite the things she'd done in her past, she was no more a whore than he was the hero of those pulp novels. She was just plain Charity and he wanted her.

He slowly undid the buttons of her bib shirt and slipped it from her shoulders. She gave him a wafer smile, tears still glistening on her cheeks.

'I love you, Rannigan. I truly do.' She lifted her chemise over her head, baring herself to him. Moonlight shined on her skin like opals and he reckoned he'd never seen anything more lovely.

No, no bar dove any longer. Only a woman. Only Charity. And more than worthy of an empty man named Wade Rannigan.

9

Darkwood appeared peaceful. The sun glittered from troughs and off windows. Frost had melted and ran in liquid diamond streaks down the glass. Townsfolk shuffled along the boardwalks, going about their business, oblivious the Devil was hiding amongst them.

A devil named Juan Rubio Latorro.

He was close; Wade could almost feel him, but where?

As they walked into the wide main street, he shot a glance at Charity, who had remained silent since she'd woken in his arms just before dawn. She knew what they were facing and knew far more was at stake than there had been two weeks ago. A future. For both of them.

He scanned the street, searching for any sign of a threat but saw none. While he doubted Latorro would move immediately, the bandit was a conundrum and Wade would keep his eyes open just in case.

Reaching the telegraph office, they stepped on to the boardwalk and he paused, gripping her hand. 'This won't take long. Ask the sheriff if he knows some reason for Latorro wantin' to stick close to town.' His face turned more serious. 'Reckon he ain't real likely to try anything in broad daylight, way you said, but watch your back all the same.'

She nodded, giving him a wry smile. 'I can take care of myself, Rannigan. Jest you recollect that.'

'That's what I'm afraid of.' He winked and stepped into the telegraph office.

* * *

Charity walked at leisurely pace along the boardwalk, a jumble of emotions washing over her. Although she had been with many men, not a one made her feel the things Wade Rannigan had last night. Their love-making had been tender and passionate, safe. And when it was over he hadn't paid her and left her feeling dirty and used and somehow less a human being. No, she had felt strangely alive and reborn and for the first time in her life she reckoned she had some hope for her future. Wade accepted who she was, what she had been. She wondered if his decision would haunt him, if he would dwell on her past and look at men on the street with suspicion and disdain. If he would look at her that way.

Hell, what are you doin'? she scolded herself. Last night was the first time she'd been with a man and felt more than disgust and self-loathing after-wards and here she was already looking for cracks where none might exist. Wade Rannigan was a hell of a man and he loved her. That was enough.

That was more than enough.

And it scared her to hell and back. When she'd set out after Latorro for killing her brother she hadn't cared whether she lived or died. She only cared about making the scalawag pay for his crime. Killing him. Although when it came down to it she hadn't been able to hit him. And it was more than just poor aim with a rifle, she was forced to admit now. Something had clutched in her soul, something that told her if she killed a man there was no going back. Maybe she just didn't have it in her that day. And now it suddenly didn't seem so important. It didn't seem worth the risk. They had a future and chasing down Latorro jeopardized that.

What if they didn't survive the encounter? Worse, what if Wade didn't? She had just found a reason to go on; if that were taken from her . . .

Shuddering, she refused to think about it. She had to focus on finding the bastard and seeing him hang. Then they could go on with their lives.

She stopped, jerking from her thoughts. A woman had stepped from an alley just a few paces ahead. She was dark-haired, her face hard, a smug expression turning her lips. She kept a hand behind her back and leaned against the corner of a building.

Charity's heart skipped a beat. She had seen the woman before, from a distance at Rannigan's camp. While she had never gotten a close look at her face, she had no doubt it was the same gal who'd put a bullet in Wade.

'Camilla de la Gato . . . ' Her voice came low, steady. She wished she had her Winchester.

'Why, sugar, you know who I am. Reckon that makes things a mite easier. I know you, too. Saw you with that Rannigan fella a few minutes ago. Figured you must be the one ridin' with him.'

Charity's gaze narrowed and she shot a glance back at the telegraph office down the street, praying Wade would walk out at any moment.

'Where's Latorro? Why ain't you with him?'

Camilla tried to look innocent. 'I escaped him. He beat me, then left and I got loose.'

Charity could see the woman's lips were swollen and a livid bruise ran along her jaw. That was one thing she wasn't lying about; Latorro had beat her all right, but she had no more escaped his clutches than El Bandolero had decided to turn himself in to the law.

'What do you want?' Charity's voice sharpened with a suspicious edge.

'I can show you where he's hid out. Then you can get your fella and kill him and help me get back to my pa.'

She was lying. No doubt of it. She might fool a man with her honey-coated words, but not Charity. She had been around enough women practiced in the art of deceit to recognize an expert and Camilla could sling with the best of them.

'You won't mind if we just wait a spell till Wade comes and we go together. I'll fetch me a rifle and the sheriff, too.'

'Why, sugar, I got me a rifle right here . . . ' She brought her hand from behind her back, holding a Winchester by the barrel. She lifted it to aim at Charity's bosom and levered a shell into the chamber. 'And I'd be right obliged if'n you'd just step into the alley with me.'

'You're working with Latorro.' Charity's accusation came cold and certain. 'You have been the whole time.'

Camilla giggled. 'Reckon he don't treat me like I am, but he will after this.' She shoved away from the corner and gestured with the rifle. 'Now git into the alley 'fore I decide findin' out why you were doggin' him ain't a reason to keep you alive.'

Camilla had already decided that; Charity saw it in her eyes. She would have shot her on the spot if she didn't have some other reason for taking her to Latorro alive. But it wouldn't take much for her to pull that trigger.

She walked forward and stepped around the corner.

A man grabbed her, throwing her hard against a building wall. She saw two men, the one jamming her to the clapboard, and a second standing off to the left, a blank expression on his face.

'Let's get her back to the shack 'fore Juan gets too riled 'bout me bein' gone so long.'

Charity thought she heard a hint of fear in the woman's voice and reckoned whatever Camilla got out of riding with the outlaw she sure as hell didn't want another beating.

The man holding her glanced back at Camilla, defiance on his face. 'Hell, Blevins said Latorro wanted us to get rid of her and that manhunter.' He looked back to Charity, hand grabbing her chin, blocky fingers digging into her flesh. 'First I want to have me a bit of fun with her.'

Camilla's face darkened and her hands went white as she gripped the Winchester tighter. 'Hell, he knew you'd never be able to get rid of them, you goddamn dimdot. He was throwing you to slaughter. This way you stay alive.'

The man's brow furrowed as he seemed to think it over. 'Well, tarnation, that don't mean I can't have me some fun with her. She's right purdy.'

'You'll do what I tell you or I'll fill you full of Winchester spit.' Camilla shifted her aim to the hardcase's back. The second hardcase remained still, face never changing expression.

The first man laughed, obviously little intimidated by a woman. 'You won't shoot me. Whole town'd come runnin' if'n you did.'

'Won't have to worry about the whole town if that manhunter comes out of that telegraph office, you sonofabitch.'

Ignoring Camilla, the hardcase turned to Charity, grinning. He pressed his mouth against hers and she tried to jerk her head away, but his blocky fingers dug deeper into her cheeks and forced her head forward.

'Hell, missy, why don't you be nice to ol' Henry and ring his bell?'

Fury overriding any fear, she jerked her knee straight up and buried it where it would do the most damage. Henry's eyes rolled up and a *whoosh* of air exploded from his lips. His hand dropped from her cheek and he took a step back, clutching at his groin.

'Bet that rang some.' A note of spite laced her voice. She balled her hand into a fist and with all her strength brought it up in a crisp arc. Knuckles collided with the underneath of the man's chin and sent him staggering backward and down. He landed in the dust, moaning, writhing in agony. 'Ding,' she added and kicked him in the ribs for good measure.

The second man, face remaining stolid, lunged, grabbing her arms and forcing her back. She tried to knee him but he was prepared for the move and the blow caught him on the thigh.

He tried to hurl her against the wall, but she grabbed two handfuls of his shirt and hung on, kicking at his shins.

'Christamighty, she's a regular hell-cat!' the man blurted and swung at her. She saw the blow coming and jerked her head. The man's fist sailed over her shoulder.

She followed up before he could set himself. Kicking him in the kneecap, she heard a satisfying crack. The man let out a bellow and suddenly an expression came to his bloodied face, one of agony mixed with shock.

Charity whirled, tried to make a run for it but the hardcase recovered enough to grab her shirt and haul her back. She twisted, attempted to scratch his eyes out, but he snapped a powerful right cross that caught her in the chin. She felt her legs go out from under her. She crumpled to the ground.

Muffled sounds thrummed in her ears, then, clearer, she heard Camilla's voice:

'Tie her across the saddle and let's git 'fore that manhunter shows up.'

'What about him?' The hardcase

nodded to his fallen companion.

Camilla glanced at the fellow, laughed. 'Leave him. He's lucky I ain't inclined to attract the attention shooting his balls off would bring. He deserves whatever he gets.'

Charity felt arms thrust beneath hers. After being dragged down the alley, she was hoisted over a saddle and lashed tight. Camilla stepped up to her, grabbing her chin and jerking her head up until their gazes met. The dark-haired woman's face wavered before her blurry vision.

'You're gonna tell Juan why you're after him, girly, and he's gonna see just how useful I am to have around.' She giggled and let Charity's head fall hard against the saddle. Blackness moved in from the corners of her mind and a moment later she was aware of nothing.

$$\star \quad \star \quad \star$$

Juan Rubio Latorro drew his Colt and blasted out one of the shack's windows.

Glass exploded and jangled to the ground. Acrid blue smoke clouded the air and filled his nostrils.

Where the hell had that *puta* gone to?

The question sent another surge of rage through his veins and he spun, firing again, again, again, and lead punched through the walls.

When the gun was empty he reloaded and shoved it into his holster.

She would be sorry indeed if she ruined his plans. Perhaps he should have killed her before he departed for the saloon yesterday. But his mind had been focused on the business at hand, his match with Rannigan and the unknown woman stalking him. Even now those men should be confronting the gringo. Of course, they would not win, not if the *señor* was as good as Juan believed him to be. In fact, if they somehow triumphed, he would be *mucho* disappointed.

He did not think he would be. No, not today. Unless Camilla had interfered.

A thought worried him: perhaps Camilla had been angrier than he believed and had gone to the man-hunter. Perhaps she had told him she was a mere victim of El Bandolero. Perhaps she would lead him back here. That was a move he had not planned for. No, even Camilla would not be so foolish. She believed she would win her game, believed he did not know her plans. But he did. He had not survived so long by being stupid. Camilla would not win. She would not best him. And she would never leave him and go back to her father alive.

But where had she gone? He did not know, but she would be back. He felt certain of it. And he would deal with her then.

For the moment he had other games to finish. McKellen. Juan had waited a very long time for revenge. McKellen would soon see the game was not ended until the checkmate was called.

The gringo had disappeared into the West after their last encounter; Latorro had searched in vain for many months, hoping to find a lead to him, but had come up empty. The defeat, a temporary one, had goaded him, gnawed away at his insides until it was the only thing he could think of.

He remembered the past well; he had relived it a thousand times over. He had worked for a small outfit then; so had McKellen. They had decided to throw in together, clean out the safe and start a spree of robberies and killing the likes of which the West had never seen. But McKellen had his own plans, and they did not include El Bandolero. Too late Juan discovered the man was nothing more than a gringo pig who intended to double-cross him and take everything for himself. But he had been too smart for the *bastardo*. Fear causes men to do unpredictable things and when Juan went after him, McKellen had pulled a derringer from nowhere and pumped two bullets into his side.

Juan had been lucky indeed to

recover from that, much the way Señor Rannigan had. The bullets had done little damage other than to his pride. But by the time he was on his feet, McKellen and his woman had vanished — with all the money.

McKellen was a fool. He believed Juan's memory and thirst for vengeance had a limit, but he was wrong. Juan had read an article in the Darkwood newspaper a few days before attempting to rob the town's bank. It told him how McKellen had taken his money and opened himself a chain of eateries back East under another name. But the paper had printed his likeness for all to see. McKellen had gone straight and forgotten all about the man he'd left for dead.

But Juan had not forgotten him.

And now McKellen and his woman, now his wife, the article had said, were returning to Darkwood to open the first in a line of new Western cafés.

And Juan Rubio Latorro would be his first customer.

A sound tore him from his thoughts and his gaze rose. His hand went to the Colt, sliding it from the holster as the door swung inward.

Camilla de la Gato stopped in the entryway, a flash of fear glinting in her eyes as she stared at the Colt aimed at her chest.

'Where have you been, *mi puta*? I have missed you.' His voice came low, measured, threatening. He had to force himself not to pull the trigger and put her out of his misery.

A man came up behind her, from the looks of him a hardcase. He had no expression on his face, even as he saw the gun.

She took a step inside. 'Just give me a chance to explain 'fore you go off all hot-headed, sugar.'

'Who is he?' Juan ducked his chin at the hardcase.

'He's one of the men Blevins hired.'

Latorro's eyes narrowed to a squint. If that man was here, something had gone wrong. And Camilla was at fault. 'Why is he here? And where is the second man?'

'Likely Rannigan or the marshal got him by now. He didn't follow orders.'

'He is not the only one, *mi niña*.' He still itched to pull the trigger. 'You must talk quickly, before I decide I do not have time to listen.'

She came inside and pointed beyond the doorway. His gaze traveled past her to see a woman draped over the saddle of a horse.

'I got that gal who was doggin' you. You still got Rannigan all to yourself, but you can see I done good, Juan.'

'Save the honey, *señorita*. I do not fall for that anyway. Perhaps I can use what you have done to my advantage. It is the only thing preventing me from filling you with lead right now.'

She cast him a glare, but remained silent. It was one of the few times since he had known her that she showed any judgement.

He looked at the hardcase, gestured with the Colt. 'Bring her in and tie her to the chair, *señor*.' The man backed out and went to the horse. Juan shoved the gun into its holster.

Camilla came up to him, running her hands across his chest and giving him a lustful smile. 'I done good, Juan. Tell me I done good.'

His eyes narrowed. 'You will never pull something that *estúpido* again, *mi niña* or I will kill you.' He shoved her away hard and she stumbled, going down. She landed on the canvas bed, a pout on her lips and hate in her eyes.

The hardcase dragged the woman into the shack and flung her on to the hard-backed chair. He laced a length of rope he'd brought with him around her hands, then around her middle and finally secured her ankles to the chair legs. Juan noticed the man had fresh bruises on his face, a swollen nose and walked with a limp. The hardcase appeared tentative around the woman while binding her, as if afraid she would suddenly spring to life.

Latorro eyed the man. 'Wait outside,

I am done with you for now.' As the hardcase stepped from the shack, Juan went to the woman, waited until he saw her eyelids flick, then slapped her. Her head jerked up, confirming she had been playing possum.

'Do not play games with me, *señorita*. You cannot win.' She glared at him, remained silent. 'Who are you, *señorita?* You look familiar, eh?'

'You go to hell, Latorro.'

'There is little doubt of that, *señorita*. But you *will* tell me who you are. I remember you from a bank, six months ago. I killed a man that day, a fool who thought to be a hero. Do you not know this man, *señorita?*'

Her lips drew tight, words barely audible. 'He was my brother, you sonofabitch.'

Latorro laughed. 'Ah, now it all makes sense. I killed your brother and now you must kill me. But that is not the way it will happen. You will see your brother again soon. I promise you that.'

'Kill her now, Juan.' Camilla pushed

herself to her feet. 'You know who she is. She ain't no use anymore.'

He looked at Camilla, shook his head. 'She will die shortly, *mi niña*. I will even let you kill her. But first I have use of her.'

A startled expression hit Camilla's face. 'Christamighty, Juan, Rannigan's gonna find out and come lookin' for her. You can't waste no time.'

Juan smiled. 'I am counting on it. It will not take him long to discover what I am after, even if he does not understand why. And if Señor Rannigan captures the other man he will be led to the saloon. But by then I will have our friend Blevins ready to deliver a final challenge to the gringo, one he cannot win.'

10

Wade walked along the boardwalk towards the sheriff's office, boots clomping in hollow rhythm on the planks, his mind still on Alejandro de la Gato, whom he'd just telegraphed.

Had the rancher hired him under false pretenses? Put him on a horse with a half-cinched saddle? If that were the case there'd be hell to pay.

He'd worry about that later. Right now he needed a plan against Latorro. He refused to stand around waiting for the outlaw to play another piece in his twisted game. Too much was at stake.

Reaching the sheriff's office, he stepped inside. The lawdog, sitting behind his desk, gazed up as Rannigan entered. A man occupied a cell, poised on the edge of the cot. An obvious hardcase, he had a foolish grin on his hard face. He held Wade's gaze.

Dread rose at the sight and it took a moment to figure out why. It wasn't so much the prisoner; it was the fact that Charity wasn't here. She should have been waiting for him.

'As I live and breathe — Rannigan!' The sheriff stood, face lighting with surprise. 'Never expected you to waltz in here alive, not after I heard Latorro was on the loose.'

Wade frowned. 'Reckon I ain't that easy to kill.'

The sheriff eyed him, brow creasing. 'Somethin' 'bout you's changed, Rannigan. Your eyes ain't so empty anymore.'

Wade nodded. 'You might say I had me a religious experience. Lady I know took me plumb to Heaven. Speakin' of which, where's Charity?'

'Who?' The sheriff looked perplexed.

'Gal I'm riding with. Latorro killed her brother. She was s'posed to be here talkin' to you about him.'

'Ain't seen no gal all mornin', Rannigan. You sure she didn't stop off somewhere first?'

Rannigan shook his head, belly filling with ice. If she wasn't here she was in trouble. He cursed himself for letting her set out for the office alone. He should have insisted they stay together, but hadn't counted on Latorro striking so quick.

'She wouldn't do that. She was comin' straight here.'

'You ain't gonna find your girly, mister . . . ' The prisoner's tone was filled with scorn.

'What do you know about her?' Wade eyed the man, took a step towards the cell.

The hardcase laughed. 'Jest that she deserves whatever the hell she gets. Goddamn hellcat.'

Wade looked back to the sheriff. 'Who is he?'

The sheriff scratched his head. 'Ain't sure yet. One of my deputies found him lyin' on the ground in an alley, clutchin' to his holy parts like they was gonna run away from home. Figured there was a story behind it and brought him in cussin' and moanin'. Was holdin' on to him till I found out who he was.'

Wade nodded. 'Go through your Wanteds. I reckon he's a hangin' waiting to happen. Latorro hired a fella to come after me while I was in Porter and I reckon this man got the same callin'. You found him in that condition I'd wager Charity got the better of him.'

The sheriff cocked an eyebrow. 'Then where is she? And why was he in the alley?'

'Likely he had help and they took her. Reckon they left him to the wolves.'

'Why the hell would they do that?'

Wade shrugged. 'Ain't sure, but I got a notion he got on someone's bad side.'

The sheriff lowered himself into his chair and pulled a stack of Wanteds from a drawer. He tossed half to Wade, who began paging through them. It took only a few moments to locate the man behind bars.

He tossed a poster at the sheriff. 'Buford Anguilera, wanted for robbery and a killing down New Mex way.'

The sheriff nodded. 'That cinches he was hired by Latorro in my mind. Birds of a feather, like they say. Why you reckon Latorro came back here, anyway?'

Wade nodded. 'I asked myself the same question. Latorro's got some reason for returning to Darkwood. You got any notion what might attract him?'

The sheriff shrugged. 'Nothin' I can think of. There's a stage arrivin' at noon but no gold on it or anything else of value. Just some restaurant fella and his wife comin' in to open up an eatery.'

Wade's brow furrowed. He couldn't see a connection, though that didn't mean there wasn't one. 'How 'bout the bank? Any larger than normal deposits?'

'Nothin'. Bank man would have alerted me if that were the case. Can't see anything that would interest a fella like that, especially since he already hit the bank in Porter. I got a deputy over there just in case.'

Wade looked over at the hardcase in

the cell, eyes locking on the man. Rage threatened to overwhelm him. If that man knew what had happened to Charity Wade was inclined to just put a bullet in him and be done with it.

'Latorro hire you to kill me?'

'*No comprendo, señor . . .* ' the man muttered in a mocking voice.

Wade's anger stepped up a notch. 'Where's Charity?' His voice came icy, steady, despite his fury.

'*No comprendo . . .* ' The man laughed. Wade resisted an urge to shoot the look off his face.

He looked at the sheriff. 'Your gallows in order?'

The man in the cell stopped smiling. Wade felt a small measure of satisfaction but until he found Charity it would not be complete.

The sheriff nodded. 'Well, reckon it was just repaired. Been itchin' to try it out.' The sheriff went to a peg and grabbed a keyring.

'Hey, what the hell you doin'?' The man's face blanched with fear. 'You can't just hang me. I'm entitled to a trial.'

The sheriff went to the cell door, unlocked it and drew his Colt. 'Your level of language comprehension sure seems to have gone up. Out or I'll give you an extra peep hole.' He gestured with the gun.

The man's gaze darted from the sheriff to Wade, but he stepped from the cell. A burst of rage overcame Wade and he swung a fist before the prisoner realized what was coming. The blow took the man square in the chin and sent him stumbling back into a table. He collapsed to the floor, wiping blood from his lips.

'You got a hell of a bedside manner, Rannigan.' The sheriff uttered a chopped laugh.

'Reckon what don't cure 'em will kill 'em,' he said with little humor. He went to the hardcase and, using his good arm, hoisted the man up, shoving him towards the door. They walked out into the street, Wade propelling the hardcase along the boardwalk.

You can't lose her, Rannigan. She's everything . . .

He forced the notion from his mind. If he dwelled on it he would come apart and right now she needed him.

A hundred yards upstreet a gallows came into view and the hardcase hesitated. Wade gave him a hard shove. A noose swung gently in the breeze.

The sheriff eyed Wade. 'She's a beauty, ain't she, Rannigan? The latest thing. Snap a man's head plumb off'n his shoulders.'

Wade glanced at the gallows, taking the lawdog's lead. It was morbid talk but any sense of compassion died the moment he learned Charity was in danger. 'Reckon she'll do the job, Sheriff. But, hell, I ain't inclined to go chasin' his head. Lots of dogs in this town I notice, though . . . '

The hardcase let out a frightened sound.

Reaching the gallows, Wade and the sheriff forced the man up the steps on to the platform.

'Got any last words?' the sheriff asked.

The hardcase licked his lips and beads of sweat coated his forehead. 'Christamighty, you can't just do this.'

Wade peered at him, then looked up at the rope. 'Where's Charity?'

The man hesitated, eyes darting. 'Christ, Latorro will kill me.'

'Either way you'll be havin' a parley with Old Nick.' Wade kept his tone steady, final.

The hardcase's gaze shifted between the sheriff and Wade. 'I dunno where she is, I swear.'

Wade gave a scoffing laugh and stepped closer, jerked the noose over the man's head. The sheriff yanked the man's hands behind his back, manacling them.

'I'm tellin' you the truth, *señor*. That gal put a knee in my saddle-bags and that *mujer*, Camilla, and the fella with me took her away.'

Wade locked gazes with the hardcase.

'Where'd they take her?'

'Ain't got any notion. I don't know where Latorro's holed up, I swear. I never even saw him.'

'Who hired you, then?' the sheriff put in.

The hardcase hesitated, muscles knotting to either side of his face. 'Blevins.'

Wade's brow furrowed. 'I heard that name before, from the fella who attacked me in Porter. Who is he?'

'The barkeep.' The sheriff's face tightened. 'Always wondered about him. If he's got some connection to Latorro he's in for a passel of trouble.'

'Why is Latorro in Darkwood?' Wade didn't expect an answer.

'Dunno. I swear, I dunno.'

Wade felt certain the man was telling the truth. He was too scared to lie. He holstered his Colt, heart picking up a beat at the thought of his next query.

'You hurt Charity?' Wade's eyes narrowed to slits.

Panic flickered across the man's face.

'Just wanted to have me a little fun with her, *señor*. I didn't mean nothin' by it.'

Wade nodded, a shadow crossing his face. He stepped over to the lever.

The man's face bleached. 'Hey, Christamighty, I told you what you wanted to know, Rannigan. You can't do this!'

'Reckon you've killed your fair share.' Wade looked at the sheriff. 'You see any reason for wastin' a jury's time?'

The lawdog slowly shook his head. 'None that I can figure.'

The hardcase let out a shriek of terror and Wade jerked the lever, cutting the sound off in mid-scream. The trapdoor beneath the man's boots fell away. A sickening crack sounded and the body spasmed.

A nervous sound came from the sheriff's lips. 'Least we won't have to go chasin' his head . . . '

Wade turned and walked down the stairs, the sheriff following.

'Obliged to you for lettin' me handle

236

that. You might have refused after I messed up with Latorro the first time.'

The lawdog nodded. 'Ain't one to judge a man on one mistake, Rannigan, and I reckon that scalawag had it comin'.'

'This Blevins will be in the saloon?'

'Most like.'

They strode along the boardwalk, faces grim, eyes hard and focused straight ahead. Rannigan fought to suppress the worry he felt over Charity. Christ, if anything happened to that gal . . .

They reached the saloon. The sheriff held his gun ready as they pushed through the batwings. Wade stopped just inside the doors. The barroom was deserted. Sunlight arced through the grime-coated windows, dust twizzling within its sepia shafts. It gave the room an eerie atmosphere that did Wade's nerves little good and filled him with a sense of suspicion. If Latorro had a notion that the hardcase had been captured by the law, he also knew the man might talk and lead them here. Was that why the place was empty?

'Best watch your back, Sheriff. I got a bad feeling about this.'

'Occurred to me Latorro was too smart to not know his man might talk.'

Wade nodded. His gaze settled on the stairs. 'You reckon he's up there?' He glanced at the sheriff.

'Could be. Damn peculiar Blevins ain't behind the counter. He lives in this saloon. He ain't never away from it.'

Wade moved towards the stairs, easing his Colt from its holster. They took the flight with caution. At the top, Wade peered down a short hall pregnant with gloom. A window at the far end was open about six inches. Dusty sunlight slanted through. Wade's gaze settled on the opening; for an instant he thought he glimpsed a dark shape on the outside stairway but it vanished so quickly it might never have been there. He passed it off as nerves, studied the hall. A series of doors led to rooms where the doves plied their trade.

Sheriff covering his back, Wade stepped to the first room, eased the door inward. Empty.

'Reckon he gave his gals the day off?' He threw a glance behind him.

The lawdog's brow crinkled. 'Ain't goddamn likely. If they ain't here, somethin's wrong.'

'Know which room belongs to Blevins?'

The sheriff ducked his chin at a door down the hall. 'That one.'

They moved down the hall, stopping before the door. Wade nodded at the lawman, who stood to the side of the door and held his gun to his cheek, barrel pointing towards the ceiling.

Wade gripped the glass knob, eased it around. Pressing himself against the wall in case a shot answered, he took a sharp breath and hurled the door inward.

Nothing.

Fingers tightening on the Colt, he chanced a look into the room.

'Christamighty . . . ' The words escaped in a whisper.

'What is it?' The lawdog kept his voice low.

Wade stepped into the room. Near the window, a man sat tied to a hard-backed chair, a bandanna cinched around his mouth. The man's sunken eyes roved, terror plain in them.

'Blevins,' the sheriff said and Wade, holstering his Colt, went to the man.

A note sticking out of the 'keep's pocket caught his attention. The barman began to jerk at his ropes and try to scream through the gag. Wade grabbed the note from his pocket, knowing his suspicions were confirmed. Latorro had figured on them coming and beat them here. He flipped open the paper, ignoring the fellow for the moment.

'What's it say?' The sheriff stepped closer, peering at the suddenly frantic barkeep. 'You just sit tight, Blevins.

You're likely in a hell of a lot of trouble.'

A shadow moved across Wade's face. 'It's from Latorro. Says I got till noon before Camilla puts a bullet between Charity's eyes.'

'Noon? That's when that stage is comin' in.'

Wade nodded, a puzzled expression on his face. 'Hell of a coincidence if you ask me.'

He stuffed the note into his pocket and reached out and jerked the gag from the bartender's mouth.

'Christ, he's gonna kill us all!' the barman shrieked, unadulterated terror in his tone.

'Calm down, Blevins.' The sheriff started around to the back of the chair to untie the man.

Blevins began struggling wildly. 'Get me out, get me out!'

Wade felt his dread step up a notch. The man was utterly terrified when he should have been relieved about being rescued.

A sound reached his ears. A horse breaking into a gallop just outside. He wondered suddenly if it held any connection to the shadow he thought he'd glimpsed on the outside stairway.

Urgency gripping him, Wade's gaze swept about the room, then stopped abruptly. 'Judas Priest . . . '

'What is it?' The sheriff, just starting to untie the ropes behind the 'keep, peered at him.

Wade's gaze settled on a strange device sitting atop the bureau, a small clock attached to some sort of spring-trap affair and wrapped about a bundle of dynamite. Realization hit him as he recollected the explosion on the trail. Latorro hadn't been anywhere near the dynamite at the time or Wade would have seen him light it. The thought hadn't occurred to him then but now it came with sudden and deadly clarity. As the notion coalesced in his mind, the hand on the clock reached the eleventh hour and stopped. A thin *click* sounded; the spring snapped closed and a spark flared into a burning flame.

'Christamighty, get the hell out of here!' Wade's yell put a startled look on the lawdog's face.

'What the hell you — '

Wade gestured at the dynamite. The fuse was too short; he would never make it across the room and stop it in time. 'Get out! He's set off dynamite!' Wade lunged for the door, the sheriff in motion an instant behind him. The barkeep started wailing in mortal terror and pounding the floor with his feet.

They plunged through thc door and hurtled down the hall, not looking back.

They didn't make it more than a few yards before an explosion tore through the room behind them. The blast shuddered the entire level and kicked them forward. Wade hit the floor and rolled, the sheriff right behind him. Wood rained to the floor as the doorframe splintered. Flames leaped from the room.

Wade pushed himself up, unsteady,

ears ringing. He stumbled to the stairs, first making sure the sheriff was on his feet and following. They went down, staggering across the barroom and out through the batwings.

Wade leaned over a rail and the sheriff collapsed against a supporting beam.

Within moments flames engulfed the saloon's upper level. Windows blew out, glass pelting the ground. Black smoke billowed up in huge tumbling clouds. Beams groaned and parts of the roof started to collapse.

Wade pushed himself from the rail and made his way out into the street, gulping deep breaths.

The sheriff came up beside him, shock on his features. 'How the hell'd he do that?'

'Got a notion he was here watching us the whole time. I reckon I heard him ride off. We couldn't have missed him by much.'

The lawman shook his head, disbelief replacing the shock. 'How'd he blow the place up that way? He wasn't in the room.'

'Some sort of timer device. Wager he had Blevins trussed up 'fore we even hanged that hardcase, then set the clock for few minutes after our arrival and left by the outside staircase at the end of the hall.'

'Hell of a way for Blevins to go,' the lawdog muttered.

Wade nodded. 'Reckon we had no choice but to leave him.'

Men had started to rush about, filling buckets from water-troughs in an effort to put out the fire, but it was a lost cause. They watched in grim silence as the saloon caved in with an explosion of sparks and black smoke, then headed back to the sheriff's office.

Wade closed the door and cast a look at the grandfather clock in the corner. 11.25. That gave him thirty-five minutes to find Charity or Camilla would kill her. At the same time Latorro would be meeting the stage and Wade couldn't be in two places at the same time. He had no notion where Charity was being held and little time to figure it out.

His gaze focused on the sheriff. 'I best start searchin' the town.'

'Hell, you ain't got the slightest notion where to start. What makes you think he ain't killed her yet anyway?'

'He don't work that way. He plays by the rules he sets. Reckon he's got a peculiar sense of honor neither of us would ever understand. I have to try finding her. I can't just sit around waitin' for her to be killed.'

The sheriff nodded. 'You don't have to convince me, Rannigan. I'll help you best I can, but I'll have to go after that stage near twelve. There's innocent folk involved and he's got some reason for hittin' it.'

'If the only thing on that stage is that fella and his wife, it's them Latorro wants. Ain't got a notion why, but you can bet it's part of some game he's got in mind.'

11.31.

Wade took a deep breath, fighting the urge to come apart. He couldn't possibly search an entire town in under half an hour. Nothing even indicated the bandit had her in Darkwood. She could be anywhere.

Goddammit, Rannigan, where's your manhunter skills when you need them? Think!

He had tracked hardcases before, sometimes against almost impossible odds, but this time he saw damn little to go on. Even if he went to where the deputy had discovered the hardcase whom they'd hanged the signs would be all but obliterated now and tracks would be scattered to the wind.

11.35

He shot a look at the sheriff, whose face was dark with hopelessness. The lawdog knew they had no chance of finding her.

It's there, Rannigan. Right in front of your face. Open your eyes . . .

He was missing something again, way he had with Camilla de la Gato's aiding

Latorro. But what? Or was he merely grasping at straws? Hoping against hope that . . .

Explosions!

When Latorro tried robbing the bank in Darkwood the day Wade captured him, he had used a gun, not dynamite. But on the trail, the robbery in Porter and in the saloon he'd used dynamite. Was that it? Was that what he wasn't seeing?

He focused on the sheriff. It was a chance, a slim one, but he had to take it.

'Where would Latorro come by dynamite?'

The lawdog scratched his chin. 'Hell, no one in town carries any since mining fell by the wayside — wait, I recollect right there's an old silver mine just outside of town. Reckon it's possible a crate or two might have been left behind.'

A spark of hope ignited inside him. 'Hell, it's better than sittin' here waitin' for her to be killed.'

'My horse is at the livery. Run over there and fetch it, another for yourself and an extra. I'll grab my deputy from the bank. If your gal's there, we might need the help.'

'Hurry.' Wade was already stepping out on to the board-walk by the time the word died on his lips.

★   ★   ★

Camilla de la Gato grabbed both chair arms and leaned close to Charity.

'Hell, girly, you ain't half as pretty as me, but I ain't like to take any chances my man'll get any hankerin' for ya. Course, you'll be dead in a few minutes so it won't a matter a lick anyhow. Juan said I could kill you at noon. I'll right enjoy it. Once a gal gets a taste for blood she just wants more and more.'

Camilla giggled and Charity saw an insane light shine in the girl's eyes. The gal was vicious as a coyote on the foam. Charity wagered she always had been and whether her father knew it when he set Wade after her was a moot point, because in a few minutes it would be over. Wade would never find her in time. Hell, he had no idea where to look. She had never really feared death, and as she poised on its threshold, she found herself still unafraid, instead filled with an aching regret that she and Wade would never have a future together.

You can't just give up! she scolded herself. That future was worth fighting for. She couldn't simply lie down and die. She was a survivor, always had been. The things life had forced upon her would have destroyed most, but not her.

Could she talk Camilla into letting her go?

How? The woman was spoiled and cruel, that was plain; she also relished the thought of committing murder. Fact, Camilla kept checking the way the sun slanted through a window to hit a stick of dynamite Latorro had braced between two rocks on the planks as an improvised sundial. By the time the shadow moved fractions of an inch more, it would be noon and Camilla would take a Winchester and put a bullet through Charity's brains.

She had to think fast. Camilla was pampered, vain, but apparently insecure where Latorro's attentions were concerned. Maybe that was the key.

'He'll just leave you, you know.' Charity kept her voice calm and she saw Camilla flinch.

'You don't know Juan, girly.' Camilla uttered a chuckle, but her words carried less confidence than they should have. That gave Charity a measure of hope. The raven-haired woman stepped back, eyeing the Winchester leaning against the wall.

'Hell, Camilla, he's always worked alone. He won't stay with you. Lots of gals in the West fall for a fella like him. He's right handsome, don't you think?'

Camilla's posture went rigid and she glared at Charity. 'Juan *needs* me. He knows that now. I done good and he'll spend more time with me.'

'You know better'n that, Camilla. Man like that's only got time for the few minutes it takes gettin' what he wants outta a gal.'

'You think so?' Camilla's voice lowered. Her lips turned in a defeated pout.

Good, the woman was falling for it. Now to just reel her in. Charity shot a glance at the dynamite; the shadow had edged hairs closer to the noon hour.

'Hell, I know so. He's got himself big plans and you'll always be on the run, least till some lawman catches up with you and stretches your neck. And if it means his gettin' free he'd leave you to the wolves.'

Camilla's hand went to her throat and worry played in her eyes. 'Juan wouldn't do that. He loves me.'

'He don't love you, Camilla. And he won't stay with one woman for long. He'll find himself a gal in some other town and you'll be dead. I know.'

Camilla's eyes narrowed. 'How do you know?'

'I know 'cause I was a whore. I seen other gals run off with fellas like him only to wind up caught by the law or found with a bullet in their skull a short spell later. Fellas find themselves a new gal 'fore the body even gets cold.'

'A whore? Yeah, I reckon I can see that.' Camilla paused, gaze flicking to the shadow. It had almost reached the noon point. 'I reckon you're right. He'd just find himself another . . .'

Charity's hope increased. 'Untie me. We'll help you, me and Wade.'

'You will?' The woman's voice sounded suddenly hopeful. 'You promise?'

'We'll get you back to your pa. We'll see to it Latorro don't ever hurt no one again.'

Camilla peered at her, a mocking look unfurling in her eyes, now, devouring any pretense of the wounded, disillusioned girl of a moment before. Charity's belly plunged. It wasn't often anyone deceived her, especially another woman. She had let her desperate hope for a future cloud her judgement and missed the fact that Camilla de la Gato was playing her for a fool.

The raven-haired girl began to laugh, the sound rising to a shrill tone. 'You got it all wrong, girly. I reckon Juan'll get tired of me soon enough, but he'll never find himself another gal, because long before he tries it I'll fill his brains full of lead. See, he don't know I'm better at the game than he is. He'll find out, though, Christ on a horse, he will.'

Charity bit back a surge of anger. It would do her no good now. She had tried and failed and now it was over. Camilla de la Gato was more than spoiled. She was a spiteful cold-hearted bitch who carried some sick attachment to Latorro, one that suited her selfish needs. Once those needs were met, never satisfied, she would move on to whatever or whoever caught her fancy. Only the thought that the girl was in for a harsh awakening if she thought she could best the outlaw gave Charity a tiny measure of satisfaction. If anyone ended up filled with lead it would be her.

Camilla went to the wall and lifted the Winchester. She stood a moment, running her fingers lovingly along the barrel.

The shadow reached the noon point.

Charity's heart stuttered a beat.

'Your man ain't a-comin', girly.' Camilla's face twisted with a bloodlust. 'I reckon I'm gonna enjoy this . . . '

She lifted the rifle to aim and sighted down the barrel. Charity closed her eyes and waited for the bullet to come.

★　★　★

They rode at a gallop for the far side of town, Wade in the lead, the sheriff and his deputy flanking his sides. His heart thundered in his throat and sweat streamed down his face.

Christamighty, Rannigan, you have to be in time. You have to do for her

255

what you couldn't for Christina.

He heeled his horse to go faster, though it was already racing at its limit. His hands gripped the reins tighter, bleaching. A knot formed in his belly and hopelessness gripped his mind. What if he were wrong? What if Latorro had gotten the explosive from another source? What if Charity wasn't at the mine and what if they were too late to stop her from being killed if she were?

The town fell away and they charged on to a hard-packed trail. Trees whipped by, blurs of green, brown, orange and red.

It had taken only a matter of moments to fetch the horses. The sheriff joined them with the deputy before he cinched the saddle on the last horse, but those saved moments were like specks of gold in a prospector's pan; they raised hope but might well turn out to be nothing more. By the time they mounted and headed for the abandoned mine, ten minutes remained till high noon.

She needs you . . .

And he needed her. He said a prayer for the first time he could recollect in years that just this once his Maker would hear the words of an unrighteous man and intervene to save Charity's life.

The trail widened and hills rose to the right. Wade spotted the mine in the distance. A shack far to the left caught his attention and he couldn't suppress a twinge of hope. Was Charity in there?

It was the sole option and letting out a sharp 'Yah!' he angled for the building.

The sheriff and deputy followed suit and within seconds they cut the distance to the shack in half.

Wade slowed his horse, leaped from the saddle, and hit the ground running before the bay came to a stop.

His hand slapped for the Colt at his hip.

Reaching the door, he gave no thought to trying the handle. He barely slowed, kicking, the momentum doubling the force of the blow. His bootheel contacted the planks with a gunshot *crack*! The door bounded inward and he followed a beat behind.

His gaze took in the scene in a flash, he saw Charity tied to a chair, eyes flying open at the sound of his entrance. Camilla de la Gato stood before her, aiming a rifle and sighting down its barrel.

The raven-haired girl started to turn and swing the Winchester towards him.

Wade brought his Colt to aim by pure instinct, triggering a shot in nearly the same instant.

Thunder filled the shack and an expression of shock and fury burst across Camilla's face. She dropped the Winchester and clutched at the hole suddenly spouting in her chest. She collapsed in a lifeless heap, blood pooling beneath her.

Wade holstered his gun and ran to Charity, relief flooding him. He pried at the knots, getting them loose. He helped her from the chair and she fell into his arms. She started sobbing, trembling, and he held her, thanking his Maker for listening to his plea.

'Hate to intrude on your reunion, Rannigan,' said the sheriff behind him. 'But we best go after Latorro while we've got the chance.'

Wade nodded, knowing they had little time, if any, to catch up with the outlaw.

'No, I'm goin' with you,' Charity said as he pushed her towards the deputy.

Wade shook his head. 'You're in no shape right now. The deputy will take you back to town. Please, Charity. No argument this time.'

She looked at him, nodded reluctantly. 'I won't argue . . . '

The deputy led her from the shack. Wade and the sheriff followed and mounted their horses.

'Lead the way, Sheriff.' Wade ducked his chin in the direction of the trail. 'You know where that stage will be comin' in.'

They gigged their horses into a gallop.

It was time to end the game.

* * *

'What you want this stage so bad for, Latorro?' asked the hardcase, as they sat their mounts at the top of the slope over-looking the trail. 'Ain't no gold on it or nothin'.'

Latorro's dark eyes settled on the man. Normally he would have shot a gringo for questioning him in such a manner but the mounting satisfaction he felt at getting another chance to finish McKellen overrode any irritation.

'Ah, *señor*, there is something much better than gold on the stage.'

The man spat, face remaining stoic. 'Hell, ain't nothin' better than gold, 'less maybe it's whores.'

Latorro shook his head. Men like the hardcase beside him did not think with their brains, only their *cojones*. A sorry life, indeed. They never knew the gratification of maneuvering pieces into a mate. 'You have much to learn, *señor*. There is a man on that stage, a man who played a game with me a few years ago. A man who thinks he's won, eh?' He cocked an eyebrow. 'He changed his name and thought that was enough. I never lose, *señor*, and that man's last sight will be of my face.'

The hardcase peered at him as though he were loco and Juan decided to put a bullet into him after they'd stopped the stage. He'd only brought him in case the law showed up.

Latorro surveyed the trail, mind drifting, wondering if Rannigan had figured out where his woman was. He doubted it, and smiled. The *señor* would never come after him with his woman in jeopardy, and it was a worthless cause to hunt for her. He would not reach her in time and he would not reach El Bandolero, either.

A sound attracted his attention. Iron tires rattling over hard-pack in the distance.

'It is time, eh?' Latorro glanced at the hardcase, then sent his horse forward and down on to the trail. The hardcase followed suit and drew up beside him.

The clamor of the approaching stage crescendoed and a moment later it was in sight. The driver, spotting the two men angled across the trail, slowed the team to a halt.

He was a grizzled, older man with missing teeth and a second skin of dust.

'No gold on this stage, mister . . . ' A tremor of nervousness laced his gravely voice. 'Nothin' else of value, neither.'

'Ah, but that is not true, *señor* . . . ' Juan drew his Colt and shot the man between the eyes. The driver tumbled off the stage to the ground, lay still.

Latorro turned to the hardcase beside him. '*Señor*, I am finished with you now . . . ' The man's face took on an expression, the first Juan had seen, one of fear.

'Hell, you can't — '

Latorro arced the gun to the man and blew him out of the saddle.

A hush descended and Juan kept his gun ready.

'Get out of the stage, Señor McKellen. Your woman, too. We have a game to finish . . . '

★   ★   ★

Wade Rannigan and the sheriff hurtled their mounts at a ground-eating pace along the trail. Wade hoped he could catch Latorro before it proved too late to save the outlaw's victim.

Ahead, three hundred yards down, he spotted sunlight glinting off something stopped in the trail. His heart leaped.

A stage. A horse with a rider stood off to the side.

Latorro!

A sudden surge of his past recklessness overriding any thought of caution, he urged the horse to go faster, cutting the distance in half within seconds.

The rider jerked around and emotion flashed across his face, a mixture of shock and anger. Latorro hadn't expected him; that was plain. He had laid his trap elsewhere, confident his opponent would remain occupied, and in the meantime he'd taken his attention from the game. He hadn't thought out all the possibilities and that was the mark of a player whose time had come to fall in defeat.

A bullet shrieked by Wade's ear and he crouched lower in the saddle.

He slowed, veering left, hand snapping his Colt from its holster and bringing it up. The sheriff arced right, getting his own gun out.

Wade caught sight of a man and woman standing between the stage and the outlaw. A glint of sunlight off metal and Latorro's head swiveled towards the couple. The man had plucked a derringer from a pocket and was jerking it towards Latorro's chest.

Latorro arced his Colt in a smooth swift motion, triggering a shot. The man skipped backwards, slamming against the side of the stage and going down face first. The woman shrieked and Latorro plucked off a second shot a beat behind. She stumbled back, grasping her belly, the scream cut short.

With the first shot, the stage team, frightened by the sudden gunfire, began to neigh, flounce their heads. By the time the woman writhed on the ground, they had worked themselves into a frenzied terror. As if guided by some unseen driver they yanked against their traces and lurched forward.

Wade had angled off to the trailside. The stage passed between him and Latorro.

The sheriff fired at Latorro. Trying to hit a stationary target while bending low and in motion wasn't as easy as the pulp novels claimed it to be. The lawdog pumped off three bullets. The first tore Latorro's hat from his head; the other two missed.

Latorro's face split in a grin and his horse danced around. He fired at the lawdog. The bullet kicked the sheriff out of the saddle. He flew backwards and landed in a patch of brush.

Wade couldn't tell how bad he was hit, but wagered it wasn't good.

The bandit let out a 'Yah!' and sent his horse down the trail.

Wade snapped off a shot, but his aim was hasty, and he missed.

He glanced at the fallen man and woman. Neither looked like they'd make it. A few feet beyond, for the first time, he noticed another man lying beside the trail, and guessed it was the second hardcase who'd attacked Charity in the alley.

Wade jerked the reins, sent his horse towards the lawdog, who had partly gained his feet and was waving Wade forward. A wound in his left side poured blood.

'Get him!' the lawdog snapped, stumbling forward. 'I ain't hit that bad.'

Wade might have disagreed, but nodded and heeled his horse into motion.

He tore down the trail, clutching tightly to the reins and his Colt. Wade wondered if the outlaw carried any more dynamite on him.

The question was answered almost instantly and not to his comfort.

An explosion tore up chunks of the trail a hundred feet ahead and a blast of air slammed into him like an invisible fist.

Through swirling clouds of dust, he caught a glimpse of the outlaw, and tensed for another blast. When no further explosions came, Wade figured Latorro had simply used a left-over stick from his saddle-bags.

The outlaw began to zigzag left then right, making himself an elusive target.

Wade closed in, and, gritting his teeth, brought his gun up.

Balancing in his saddle, he fired, trying to hit the back of the outlaw's weaving shape.

The bullet missed. Wade drew aim the best he could, and fired again.

He missed the outlaw but lead sizzled by the horse's flank close enough to cause the animal suddenly to fight its master.

Latorro struggled to keep the bay heading forward. Wade's former horse didn't spook easy, but he reckoned that with all the gunfire and the explosion the gelding's nerves were frayed and it wouldn't take a hell of a lot more.

Wade triggered three shots, hoping to come close enough to booger the animal into throwing Latorro. One of the bullets whistled past the bay's ear.

The mount, skittish already, skidded to a halt and began to buck and rear. Latorro might have been a master bandit and chess player but it instantly became plain he was no horseman. His boot wrenched out of a stirrup and he flew through the air and down, hitting the ground hard. The horse vanished in a cloud of dust down the trail.

Wade aimed for another shot as the outlaw rose. He squeezed the trigger.

The hammer fell with a hollow *clack*.

Cursing, Wade pulled hard on the reins, drawing up and leaping from the saddle.

On his feet now, Latorro plunged

into the woods, his shape soon lost amongst the trees. Wade heard him thrashing through brush. Low hills studded with trees and boulders rose in that direction and Latorro was obviously heading for them.

Wade angled left, sheltering himself behind a huge pine and reloading. He chanced a look, hearing the outlaw's movements far to his left, but couldn't see him. Crouching, he darted from tree to tree, heading in the direction of the sounds.

A blast rang out and a bullet shrieked inches from his face. Wade lunged for the shelter of a boulder, getting behind it. Another shot followed, chipping a shard of stone loose.

'You cannot win, *señor!*' The bandit's voice came in a shout, taunting. 'Say your prayers now.'

Sweat trickled down Wade's face. 'You best do the same, Latorro. I ain't takin' you in alive this time.'

A harsh laugh echoed through the air. 'I am not a righteous man, *señor*, or has that not yet occurred to you?'

'Reckon you might change your mind once you end up facing Old Nick.'

Wade had to keep him talking, figure out from which direction the outlaw's voice was coming. Sound echoing from the rocks and trees was deceptive, but he thought he placed the source about thirty yards to the right. A cluster of low trees studded the hillside there.

'I would only beat him at his own game, *señor*. You must know that.'

A thin smile turned Wade's lips. Latorro liked to brag damn near as much as he liked to see everything as a game.

Wade, crouching, moved left, exposing himself for only a moment as he made it to the shelter of a large tree. If he could circle in back of the bandit, surprise him, he had a chance.

'Camilla's dead, Latorro.' He hoped the announcement would divert the bandit's attention, focus it on something other than Wade's maneuver.

Silence came back and a dim

suspicion rose in Wade's mind. That wasn't like Latorro.

The reason became painfully obvious a moment later. Something hit the back of his head and he went stumbling, senses reeling, gun flying from his fingers. Wade struggled to keep his feet, failed, went down.

'You are not an experienced player, *señor*. Do you think I would have survived this long if killing me were so easy?'

Wade looked up and through blurry vision saw the man standing above him, a grin on his face. The Colt in Latorro's hand centered on Wade's chest. The bandit had accomplished the very thing Wade intended, maneuvered around and taken Wade by surprise. Now his gun lay ten feet away and he would be dead before he made a move for it.

'I told you to say your prayers, *señor*. You cannot beat me, no one can . . .'

'The hell they can't!' a voice snapped out and Wade's gaze jerked to a spot beyond the bandit. Latorro twisted, shock hitting his features.

At the edge of the trail stood Charity, a Winchester jammed to her shoulder. She pulled the trigger and a shot thundered through the trees.

The outlaw had turned just enough to avoid being drilled through the back. Lead punched into his shoulder and his Colt flew from his grip. He staggered sideways and Wade, forcing himself to act, seized the opportunity and scrambled towards his gun.

Something hit him with the force of a bull slamming into a barn door. He went over, the outlaw coming down on top of him.

It was the only move the man could have made to preserve his life and proved him to be the master player he claimed himself to be. Charity would have buried him with a second shot or Wade would have reached his gun and finished the job. Even wounded, the bandit thought clearly and seized the only possible defense. He had checked the king.

They went over, the outlaw using his good arm in an effort to pound Wade's head into the ground. Both men had near useless shoulders, though Latorro's streamed blood and if that happened long enough he would weaken.

Kicking out, Wade endeavored to throw the outlaw off of him. The bandit, unable to keep his balance, went sideways.

Wade tried to scramble up, reaching his knees just as the outlaw reared up and, with one hand, grabbed hold of Wade's shirt.

He jerked back, but the hardcase held on. Both men struggled to their feet.

Wade snapped a short uppercut that connected with the outlaw's chin; a blank look crossed Latorro's dark eyes for an instant. The blow would have been enough to finish most men but the outlaw shook it off and swung Wade around, keeping the manhunter between himself and Charity's rifle.

Wade brought a knee up as the outlaw pressed close, but it missed, bouncing off the man's muscled thigh. The outlaw snapped his forehead forward, hit Wade square in the mouth. Blood sprayed from his lips and agony rang through his jaw.

Latorro let go and dove for Wade's gun, which lay only a few feet away.

A shot came from Charity's Winchester but the bullet missed by a couple feet, burying itself in the ground.

Wade moved on pure instinct. He lunged at the outlaw just as the man made a grab for the gun, coming down on top of him.

Both touched the weapon and tried to get it into their grip.

Throwing all his weight forward, he pinned Latorro to the ground. He struggled to keep the tenuous hold he gained on the weapon, while Latorro fought to pull it away, turn the barrel towards the manhunter and get his finger around the trigger. Wade strained to turn the muzzle back towards the bandit.

Their eyes met, locked.

'You lose, *señor* . . . ' Latorro triggered a shot.

The blast stunned Wade's ears. For an instant, he expected to feel lead sear through his belly.

But didn't. He saw a startled expression flash into the outlaw's eyes, sheer disbelief.

'*Señor* . . . no . . . ' the bandit mumbled and blood bubbled from his lips. 'I always . . . win . . . ' His eyelids fluttered and his head lolled sideways.

Gasping, drenched in Latorro's blood, Wade pushed himself off the bandit and gained his feet. A huge hole showed in the outlaw's stomach, pumping blood.

Wade stumbled back a step, shaking with exhaustion and relief.

Charity rushed up to him, dropping her rifle and throwing her arms about him.

'You were s'posed to go back to town

with the deputy ... ' he said, no condemnation in his voice. She had saved his life. Again.

She gave him an easy smile. 'You didn't honestly think I'd listen?' She chuckled. 'I reckon that deputy was right happy to be rid of me and tell me where the stage was comin' in by the time I got done bitchin' at him.'

A grim hush fell over the woodland and they gazed at the dead form of Juan Rubio Latorro. Wade reached into his pocket and pulled out the white queen. He tossed it beside the bandit.

'Checkmate,' he whispered.

★   ★   ★

A blanket of slate gray hid the sun and a chilly wind kicked up fallen leaves as Wade rode into the de la Gato ranch compound. He rode at a funeral pace, the slow burn of anger in his veins at having been deceived and played for a fool mixing with a grim sense of pity for the man whose daughter's homecoming would be a solemn occasion indeed.

Behind him, a buckboard followed, driven by Charity, whose face was set in mournful lines.

The compound was large, semi-circular and littered with outbuildings, corrals and a huge shiplap main house with multiple levels.

A rich man's dream.

Sometimes dreams weren't so far from emptiness, he reckoned.

The door opened as they approached. Charity angled off to the side, while Wade kept straight on. A man stepped out on to the porch and came down the stairs. Reining up, Wade eyed him.

'You've found my daughter?' Alejandro de la Gato was a beefy, dark-complexioned man with an arrogant turn to his face and superiority in his slate-colored eyes.

Wade gave a somber nod. 'I found her. You weren't quite honest with me, though, were you?'

The older man's gaze narrowed and bluster came into his voice. 'What the devil are you talking about?'

'You sent me after your daughter knowing full well Latorro didn't kidnap her. You never paid any ransom, either. She went with him willingly and damn near killed me.'

'That's your word against mine and I doubt you have enough power to come out on top even with your reputation, Rannigan. Now I demand to know where she is.'

Wade frowned. He reckoned he'd been hoping for some redeeming quality in the man, and couldn't deny he was disappointed when none showed. 'I always fulfill my promises, de la Gato. I said I'd bring her home and I did.' He ducked his chin towards the buckboard. Charity climbed from the driver's seat and came towards Wade. He reached down and helped her into the saddle behind him.

Alejandro de la Gato's gaze went to the back of the buckboard and he suddenly began to scream. He rushed over to it, face draining white. A blanket-covered body lay in the back. The man, utter defeat in his eyes looked back at Wade.

'Why?' he mumbled. 'Why is she dead?'

'Devil always collects his marker when you play with other folks' lives, de la Gato. Reckon I rightly don't know what made her do the things she did or hook up with a fella like Latorro in the first place. Maybe you got the answer to that.'

Rage reddened the rancher's beefy face. 'You're sayin' I'm responsible for this? That I killed her? I've shot men for less than that, Rannigan.'

Wade shrugged, a heaviness in his shoulders that came straight from his soul. 'I'm sorry for your loss . . . ' He reined around and heeled his horse into an easy gait away from the compound. A backward glance told him de la Gato would present no hindrance to their departure. The man had collapsed sobbing over the blanketed body of his daughter.

'Hell of a thing,' Wade muttered and felt Charity clutch tighter to him. Latorro and Camilla were gone, as were another man and his wife, both murdered by El Bandolero. Wade reckoned he'd never know why the outlaw had killed those two. The sheriff would pull through and Wade was glad of that. The lawdog was a fine man.

He forced his thoughts on to happier notions. It was time to leave the past and ride into the future.

'I noticed a little church on our way here . . . ' He held his voice steady but it was a chore. His belly fluttered.

'You askin' me to marry you, Wade Rannigan?' A hint of excitement claimed Charity's voice.

'Reckon I am.'

She clutched to him tighter and began to cry with tears of joy and he knew he had his answer.